Praise for The Longest Man-Made Beach in the World: Biloxi Stories

The Longest Man-Made Beach in the World reminds me why I love short stories. These are tales of families in peril—the missing, the dead, the near-dead—and the people trying to hold everything together (often children, the least and strongest among us). I could see myself in every character. Setting is the highlight here: the heavy air, white sand beaches with water unfit for swimming, and the region's complicated history of racial injustice and neglect. An exceptional debut.

—Mary Miller, author of *Biloxi: A Novel* and *Always Happy Hour: Stories*

Amelia Franz's debut story collection, *The Longest Man-Made Beach in the World: Biloxi Stories*, is a secular litany of prayers for the impoverished and grieving, the wounded or wounding child, the abused wife and mother, the hapless man with dementia, the brother blighted by old guilt. Brilliant stories of sorrow, regret, resilience and stubborn hope, reminiscent of John Steinbeck, James Agee and Carson McCullers. These are searing evocations of individuals and families fighting steep odds, compelled by universal longings, scarred but seeking grace. A masterful, memorable debut.

—Melissa Pritchard, author of *Flight of the Wild Swan* and *Palmerino*

Amelia Franz knows "place"—its aromas, its accents, its palettes, its people. With deceptively simple, clean prose, she immerses the reader in the backwaters of the Mississippi Gulf Coast, a place that is anything but simple. These stories remain unexpectedly with the reader long after they've turned the page—like sand in one's shoes or glass shards in a tire.

—Jen Michalski, author of *All This Can Be True*

A stunning debut: Amelia Franz skillfully delivers a suite of sublime, tender short stories, perfect as pebbles on a Gulf state beach. Biloxi, Mississippi haunts the novel, folding its wings to observe the fraught, intimate vignettes that unfurl in this slim collection. Franz's is the valiant new voice that the longest man-made beach in the world deserves.

—Meri Robie, author of *Wildflowers*

In this anthology of 11 tales ranging from 5 to 15 pages each, Franz explores the lives of ordinary people who reside in and around Biloxi. They struggle with personal weaknesses, unresolved tragedies, and the persistent sense of longing that comes from the fact that Biloxi is home to the world's "longest man-made beach," with all that this implies about a greater, more natural world somewhere beyond the town limits ... All of these stories are markedly, sometimes startlingly spare, which underscores Franz's deft ability to convey whole lives and worlds with minimal, very controlled brushstrokes ... a strong, vivid batch of tales.

—*Kirkus Reviews* (Verdict: "Get It")

The Longest Man-Made Beach in the World

Biloxi Stories

Amelia Franz

WATERTOWER PRESS
Baltimore

Published by Watertower Press, Baltimore, Maryland

ISBN: 9798985598278

Biloxi, Mississippi is a real city, but this book is a work of fiction. Names, characters, events, businesses, and situations are products of the author's imagination or used fictitiously. These stories are not intended to depict any person, living or dead.

*Be kind, for everyone you meet is fighting a
battle you know nothing about.*

—Variously Attributed

Contents

The Gospel Voice on Your AM Dial

AT 10:30 THAT MORNING, Mama started calling around.
First it was the hospitals, then Micky Guidry, Daddy's fishing
buddy since Biloxi High. Next, my Uncle Cal, then Uncle
Doug in Pascagoula. She even called two of his coworkers
from the marina. As she talked, she doodled his name, Larry,
on the back of an envelope, then circled it in pencil over
and over, until the letters seemed to stare out of a deep cave
or a fat, black tornado. I sat on a stool at the breakfast bar
holding the Bread of Life, which wasn't bread at all but a
loaf-shaped plastic container that held printed Bible verses in
assorted colors. I was shuffling the verses around, just to have
something to do with my hands.

But nobody knew Daddy's whereabouts or why he hadn't
come home the night before. Mama hung up the phone, walked
over to the percolator, and poured herself a cup of coffee. She

stirred in milk and sugar, then stared out the window between curtains she'd sewn herself long ago, the fabric patterned with cornflower blue Dutch boys and Dutch girls in wooden clogs, tulips and windmills in the background, and a faded, once-cheery pompom fringe along the bottom.

Two weeks earlier, it was him who'd stood in that spot, pouring bottles of tequila down the drain, *glug glug glug,* promising he was done with the stuff for good and we could take that to the bank. When the two of us went fishing three days later, his hands were so shaky, I had to bait his hook. *Too much coffee,* he said, as I took the shrimp and skewered it. *Shouldn't have had that second cup.* I knew what the shaking meant but hadn't answered, only stared into the dark water below, foaming and swirling around the bridge's barnacle-crusted pilings.

I set the Bread of Life on the counter, next to my Corn Flakes and Tang.

"He could have called, at least. Don't cost but a quarter."

"I know, Baby."

"I'm twelve years old. I'm not a baby."

She nodded absently and took one last sip of coffee, then poured the rest down the drain. She walked over and took her purse from the sideboard and her keys from a cut glass candy bowl near the door that led to the carport, then announced she was going out to look for him.

"Try not to worry," she told me. "I'll be back as soon as I can."

But I couldn't just sit there and wait. "I'm coming, too."

To my surprise, she didn't argue, just said to use the bathroom first and that she'd be waiting in the Pinto. But when I climbed into the passenger seat and she turned the key in the ignition, the engine only made a *tickticktick*.

"It's the battery," she groaned.

So she popped the car in neutral, and the two of us eased it from the carport, down the sloping driveway and into the street. Next door, Mr. McNair was out watering his flowers. Seeing us, he turned off the hose and came over to help steer the car alongside the curb. He was retired military from Keesler Air Force Base, a widower whose wife had died of stomach cancer and who now spent most of his days shearing his boxwoods into perfectly round balls, mowing his lawn into ruler-straight light and dark green stripes, or fussing needlessly with low-maintenance azaleas and hibiscus. Once the car was next to the curb, he went back to his house, then drove over in his pickup to give us a jump.

As he raised the car's hood, Mr. McNair glanced at me. "How you doing, Stevie?"

"Okay." I hadn't spoken to him for months now, not since I came home from school to find Daddy in his front yard, red-faced and slurring his words, accusing the man of not returning a borrowed flounder gig, which he'd later remember he'd loaned to a different neighbor. Mama was still at work at the hospital and wouldn't be home for another hour, at least. I could see Mrs. Helen and Mr. Buddy across the street, watching the show through their picture window. I wanted to die of embarrassment. Before that day, Mr. McNair and I used to talk now and then, about how the Saints were playing and what Dick Nolan might be able to do, now that he'd taken over as head coach from Hank Stram. About California, where Mr. McNair was from, and how I really ought to see it one day because there was nothing in the world like the Pacific Ocean. He'd let me pick dewberries from the bushes that grew along his back fence and ask me how school was going, even loaned me paperback westerns to read. But since the flounder gig incident, I had avoided our neighbor, looking away if I saw him in his yard.

When the Pinto roared to life, Mr. McNair unclamped the red and black cables from the terminals and told her to drive it around twenty minutes or so. "Just to make sure it's fully charged. It'll be alright for a few days, I think, but you'll need to replace that battery pretty soon."

Neither of them mentioned Daddy. She thanked Mr. McNair over and over, but I noticed she didn't look him in the eye, either.

***

AND THEN, BAR BY bar, we worked our way down pre-casino Biloxi Beach from Beauvoir, historic home of Jefferson Davis, to the Biloxi-Ocean Springs bridge. While I waited in the car, she marched into places with names like Kandy's and The Lucky Lounge. All I could think was how ridiculous my mother looked, red hair piled high in that pentecostal pouf, blue jean skirt way past her knees. I wondered if she'd ever even been inside a bar.

She carried a woven wooden basket purse with a curved handle and hinged lid. Inside it, she'd put a framed five-by-seven Sears family portrait, the most recent picture of Daddy she could find. If a bar was still closed, she banged the front door with her fist or the flat of her hand until someone eventually answered. At one place, a shirtless man flung open the door, and out lunged the biggest German shepherd I'd ever seen, snapping and slobbering and growling until the guy yanked it back by the leash. We must have checked fifteen or twenty bars. I lost count. But each time, she went in alone and came out alone, quick little humiliated steps back to the Pinto with her head down.

***

AT SOME POINT, WE stopped at the pay phone between Krispy Kreme and Rax Roast Beef and called home, on the off chance he'd made it back. She stood in the booth, letting it ring and ring, and when there was no answer, we went into Rax to sip fountain drinks and cool off. It was May, and the car's a/c was running warm. Daddy kept saying all it needed was a can of freon, but somehow he never found the time to take care of it.

They were running a promotional celebration that day, and one of the Rax workers wore the green and brown costume of Uncle Alligator, the chain's mascot. He was handing out helium balloons to all the little kids, but since the head contained no eye holes, another employee—a pimply-faced teenaged boy—had to lead the blind and shuffling alligator around. The boy was too fast sometimes, not careful enough, and the alligator kept bumping into tables and chairs. I was small for my age and half-afraid they'd think I was a little kid, too, and offer me a balloon. But before they could make it to our table, I heard Mama's name called.

"Linda! Linda Pruitt!"

It was Miss Barb. They used to work together in Bath and Bedding at JCPenney, before Mama took a secretarial course and got her job at the hospital. Miss Barb was a twice-divorced former Catholic who wore skimpy clothes and heavy makeup. Some at our pentecostal church referred to women like her as Jezebels, but the way she lived and dressed never seemed to bother Mama. Late one night, I woke to the sound of a woman sobbing. When I tiptoed out of my bedroom and down the hallway, it was Miss Barb's mascara-striped face I'd seen at our kitchen table, Mama consoling her because her boyfriend, Jack, had left her for a younger woman.

"What are y'all up to today?" Miss Barb said, walking over with a wide, lipsticked grin.

"Aw, you know. Just this and that. Out running errands," Mama said. For no reason, she picked up a bottle of ketchup, then set it back down on the red Formica tabletop.

"Well, I haven't seen you in a blue moon. And Stevie's just getting so big! How are things?"

"Fine." Mama's smile was tight-lipped and didn't reach her eyes.

"Well, just let me go order, and I'll be right back. We need to catch up, girl."

But Mama glanced at her watch and said that, unfortunately, we had to get going. She sure was sorry, and they definitely needed to get together for coffee one of these days.

On our way out of Rax, she slipped on her shades, the tortoise shell frames so large they covered nearly half her face, only the pink tip of her nose protruding. We didn't mention Miss Barb as we walked back to the car. We didn't mention anything at all for a while, just worked our way down Highway 90 in grim silence. On one side stood white-columned, antebellum mansions gazing out at the Gulf from deep lawns shaded by ancient live oaks. But the other side, the beach side, was a jumble of bars and motels and strip clubs and souvenir shops selling large, baby-oiled seashells shipped in from someplace far more tropical than Biloxi, Mississippi.

We even looked for him on the beach. This was years before Mayor Blessey banned glass, and people were always slicing their feet open on broken bottles, so we kept our shoes on and slogged through the sand. There were kids tossing beach balls and tourists bouncing along over the waves in rented catamarans with striped sails. There was the Bobbie's String Bikinis van, The Beach Arcade, and a dead dolphin swarming with flies, its mouth stretched in a horrible smile. But there was no passed-out father in the sand.

Finally, we made it back to the car and sat on a nearby bench to rest, the Highway 90 traffic whizzing past. I peeled off my socks and shook them out, wiped the sand from between my toes the best I could. The socks were still gritty, but I put them back on. My sweaty tee shirt clung to my back. Overhead, a plane was dragging a banner that read MARRY ME DENISE, and I wondered why in the world anybody would ever want to get married. But I knew why. Sometimes they had to. It was why my parents had married, because of me. I'd once overheard my Grandma Ruth say so during an argument at her house in Ocean Springs. She'd said if Mama had just known how to keep her legs shut in high school, her entire life could have been a whole different story.

"I ain't never getting married," I said.

Mama's face was red from the heat, and she fanned herself with her hand.

After a few seconds, she said, weakly, "Marriage can be a beautiful thing."

"I just want to go home. This is stupid."

"We will, Baby. There's just one more place I want to check."

"I'm twelve years old. I'm not a baby."

***

So WE DROVE ON, past the Eight Flags of Biloxi and the sign boasting of the longest man-made beach in the world. Near the Small Craft Harbor, she made a sharp right turn at Jerry's Jackpot Lounge. It might have been the ugliest bar in Biloxi—a squat, flat-roofed building made of cinder block painted olive green, with a letterboard sign out front that read FABULOUS

FLOOR SH W. Posters of puffy-haired women with large breasts and spray-paint-covered nipples lined the windows. A man in a long-sleeved shirt, odd on a ninety-degree day, stepped out of the place and walked over to a parked car, reached in, and slipped something in his pocket. As we parked, he gave us a long, sideways look, then went back inside. I had a bad feeling about the place.

"Don't go in there," I said. I actually reached out and grabbed her wrist.

"Just sit tight, Son. I won't be long."

I let her go, but I'd had enough of sitting tight. I got out and kicked a beer can around the lot.

There were a dozen or so cars, one of them a beat-up old Pontiac the red-orange color of mercurochrome, with a constellation of rust holes along the passenger side. The rear window was halfway down, and as I passed, I noticed a little girl lying on the back seat. Her dress was hiked up around her waist, panties showing and bright red mosquito bites dotting her legs. She sat up, panting in the heat, and stared at me. Her hair was a small, dark helmet plastered to her head with sweat. I stared back, unsure what to say.

Seconds later, the door opened, and Mama came out of the bar, alone again. I called her over. "There's a little kid out here in this car."

Mama talked to her through the window. "How long have you been out here, Hon?"

The girl, who said her name was Kim, shrugged and said she didn't know because she'd been asleep. We unlocked and opened the door and told her to come on out and cool off.

But Kim shook her head. "Naw. Mama's in there with her friends. If I get out, she'll beat my ass."

The girl wasn't our responsibility, and a small, selfish part of me almost wished we would just leave. But I knew it wasn't going to happen.

"Well, Miss Kim, I'm gonna go in and find your mama. Stevie'll stay here with you."

After she left, Kim lay back down on the seat and sucked her thumb, then sat up and spoke to me for the first time.

"Your mama's nice."

"I guess."

"Mine ain't."

And a couple of minutes later, Mama came out of the bar and headed our way with a tumbler of ice water and a ratty-haired, glassy-eyed lunatic on her heels.

"Fuckin' bitch! Mind your own fuckin' business!" the woman bellowed. Mama walked faster, but Kim's mother ran around, blocked her path, and slapped the glass from her hand. It shattered on the patchy asphalt, and a trickle of blood ran down Mama's leg and into her white Keds.

I did not even think, just charged the woman, roaring like a maniac and waving my arms.

"Steven! Get back in the car!"

But there was no need. To my amazement, the woman actually looked frightened, or maybe only startled. She glanced down at the glittering shards, ran a hand through her hair, and muttered *shit*. She slammed Kim's door shut and went around the front of the car to the driver's side. The Pontiac cranked on the third try, and off they went, tires slinging sand and loose gravel back at us. Through the rear window, we could see Kim watching us, her face resting on balled fists. We watched that face recede, smaller and smaller, until they turned onto eastbound 90 in a cloud of gray-blue exhaust.

Mama stepped carefully around the broken glass, then took a Kleenex from her purse and dabbed at the nick on her ankle. She tore off a dime-sized piece of tissue and left it stuck there. The sight of blood had never bothered me in the past, but it bothered me now. I felt a little queasy—and for the first time all day, angry. I found it hard to be mad at my father, even harder to stay mad at him. But I was furious now. It felt wonderful.

"He's a dickhead!" I yelled, the first time I'd ever cursed in front of her. "He's an alcoholic!" It was the first time I'd ever said that, too. I stood there waiting for her to tell me I was wrong. She didn't.

Back in the Pinto, she gripped the wheel so hard her knuckles popped up knobby and white. And then, I couldn't believe it. She punched in the cigarette lighter. We never used the cigarette lighter. I didn't even know how I knew it was a cigarette lighter. She rummaged around in her purse and whipped out a pack of Marlboro Lights like it was nothing. When the lighter popped, she held the glowing orange ring to the cigarette and took a long, deep, squinty drag, then blew the smoke expertly out the other side of her mouth. I knew she used to smoke years ago, before she got saved and joined the church. But smoking was against church teachings, and worse, it was a sin because the body's the temple of the Holy Ghost. I forgot all about the woman and her little girl. I forgot about Daddy and where he might be. I just sat there, watching her smoke.

"I didn't know you smoked."

"I don't."

After a little while, I asked, "What now?"

She took one last drag and flung the cigarette out the window, then swiveled around in her seat and looked me in the face.

"Stevie, the Lord tells us in His Word, if we've got faith

the size of a mustard seed, we can say to a mountain, *get up and move*." She pinched her thumb and pointer finger together, as if they held the tiny seed. "Do you believe that, Son? Are you ready to stand on the promises with me? Can we pray together, right now?"

Behind the bar was a vacant mud and shell lot where a flock of gulls flapped and swooped and screamed, ripping apart a small blue crab. Past that lay the beach and the Mississippi Sound. The water was putty-colored, tipped with whitecaps that winked at me—here one second, gone the next. Out in the channel, a buoy rocked from side to side, something in that motion seeming to mock the two of us.

I didn't know what I believed. I didn't know if I was really even saved. I liked the Psalms, the parables, the Old Testament stories. I liked Brother Cecil, our pastor. But secretly I suspected the whole thing was made up because nobody walked on water or rose from the dead. But I bowed my head while she begged the Lord to hold my father in the palm of His hand and let no harm befall him. And keep that poor woman and her little girl safe, too.

And then we drove to the police station.

***

THE SERGEANT'S DESK WAS topped with a thick layer of glass he kept tapping his pen on, *blick blick blick.* We'd have to wait until twenty-four hours had passed before filing a missing persons report, he told us right away, and Daddy had only been gone since six last night. But he doubted it would even come to that. Daddy was probably just sleeping it off somewhere or maybe back home already, waiting for her with the biggest bunch of doghouse roses she'd ever seen in her life.

Not far from his desk, two other officers were eating wafer sandwich cookies and laughing about a TV show. Mama shut her eyes and rubbed her forehead with her fingertips, pressing hard, the way she did with a migraine.

"You're not hearing me, sir. What if Larry's hurt? Or if he's got himself mixed up in some kind of gambling mess? Y'all know what goes on down there." She jerked her thumb in the direction of the beach.

To which he replied that he'd lived on the coast all his life and knew very well what went on down there, but we were not going to get ahead of ourselves. "If you don't hear from him by six on the dot, just come on back. We'll do the paperwork then and get the ball rolling." His eyes cut over to me, then again to her, as if one more thought had just occurred to him.

"No disrespect or nothing, but could your husband be with, you know, a friend?"

She stared at her lap. "No sir," she said in a small voice.

"Are you sure?"

"Very sure."

He glanced at his watch. "In that case, I reckon we're just about done here."

"But I know something's wrong," she flared up. "I wish you'd just listen to me. I'm telling you, Larry's never stayed out all night before. That's just not something he does."

He sighed and tapped his pen on the glass, *blick blick blick.* "Unfortunately, Hon, there's a first time for everything."

At this grim truth, the three other officers burst into laughter again, much louder now. One of them was impersonating Fred Sanford from *Sanford and Son*, when the old man fakes a heart attack, looks up towards heaven, and shouts that he'll be joining his dead wife soon. The female officer bent over and slapped her knee. I knew they weren't laughing at us, but that's what it felt like.

Mama stood up so fast, she knocked over a Styrofoam cup of coffee with her elbow. It streamed all over the glass, and then the sergeant was snatching up all his things, his paperwork and stapler and small framed photos. The female officer rushed to the desk with paper towels and began mopping up the coffee, and then he walked around the desk to face us. But to my surprise, the man didn't even seem angry about the spilled coffee. He looked at Mama as if she were only a fussy toddler who'd missed her nap.

He clapped me hard on the shoulder. "Take good care of your mother. Can you do that for me, Buddy?"

I just wanted to get out of there, but Mama had one more surprise in store. She stepped right up to the officer, only inches from his chest and his shiny badge, inches from the fat, silver revolver on his hip. He was a head taller, so she had to look up to meet his eyes. I thought my heart would stop. But I'll always remember that the man took one small step back.

"Mister," she said, in a tone I'd never in my life heard her use. "You don't know your behind from a hole in the ground."

Nobody was laughing now. The place fell silent. The officers watched us turn around and walk out the double doors with our heads high. We did not look back.

"And my name ain't Buddy," I added, not quite loud enough to be heard.

But as our luck would have it, the Pinto's engine only made the familiar *tickticktick* when she turned the key in the ignition.

"Oh, shoot." She closed her eyes and rested her forehead on the steering wheel.

We both knew we'd just have to suck it up. Walk back into the station, humble ourselves, and ask for a jump. And we did, but not right away. First, we sat there a good, long while in the heat, just dreading it. But then, of course, we dragged ourselves up those steps and through those doors again, feeling like a couple of very minor criminals.

"Excuse me, ma'am," she said to the woman behind the front desk. "We seem to be having some car trouble."

The sergeant heard us and came over. Maybe I only imagined his tiny smirk.

After the battery was charged and one of the officers unclamped the cables, we thanked him and wished him a good day. And then, since there was nowhere else to look and nothing at all to do now but wait, we headed home to D'Iberville.

***

WE CAUGHT THE DRAWBRIDGE over Back Bay. The lights flashed, the bell clanged, and the red-and-white striped arm lowered in front of the bumper. The deep mechanical whirring began, and the center sections of the bridge rose until they pointed to the sky. Mama switched on the radio to her favorite station: AM 1200, "The Gospel Voice on Your AM Dial." She took out a cigarette and lit it, then rested her arm out the window, tapping now and then with her pointer finger. The ash flurried over the guard rail and the bay.

The DJ said this next song was a special request, and whenever he heard it, he just wanted to get down on his prayer bones and thank the Lord for his tender, loving care. It was "Consider the Lilies," a church song I'd heard many times. The words were based on verses from the Book of Luke, when Jesus tells his disciples they don't need to worry because the flowers don't worry what to wear, do they? And the birds don't worry what they'll eat. And if our Heavenly Father cares for birds and insects, even grasses of the field, just imagine how much He cares for you and me.

There were things I wanted to say. I wanted to tell her I thought she was brave. But somehow I knew I would never tell her, and then the moment was already gone. The sailboat's silver mast appeared on the south side of the bridge. The sections lowered and locked into place. The red-and-white arm rose, and then our tires were humming over the steel grid.

Sharp Dressed Man

IT WAS A BOX, and who had three thousand bucks to spend on a box? Her daddy would have said, just wrap me in a bed sheet and drop me in a hole. All the same, Julie let herself be led around the burgundy-carpeted showroom, pretending to consider all the choices and options: The Oxford, The Wellington, The Legacy, The Elite. Stainless steel and bronze, fine hardwoods in oak, mahogany, and cherry, overhead lights positioned to make the polished wood glow. It was a box. Yet the lock and rubber gasket seal of the Oxford caught her eye. She thought of a coffin she'd seen unearthed after Katrina—so small, it must have held a child, perched sad and surreal on a pile of debris near what was once the Biloxi Beach Arcade, half-open and rusted through in that mess of lumber and moldy insulation and raw poultry strewn from shipping containers tossed around like Coke cans by the thirty-foot wall of water.

"Did you have anything in particular in mind for your dad?" The tone of the funeral director's assistant was practiced, reverential. There were more questions. Was she interested in a full couch or half couch, meaning a one-piece or two-piece lid?

"Half," Julie said. She glanced down at the FTC-mandated casket price list she'd been given in advance. "But I was thinking of something, you know," she paused, "simpler."

"Oh sure, sure. Absolutely. No problem at all. Why don't we take a look at our, um, particleboard line?" The gray-suited man indicated a small, adjoining space off the main showroom floor. "Less expensive but just as elegant. Any one of them would make a fine resting place for Mr. Malavich."

"Maravich."

"Maravich, sorry. Slip of the tongue."

That slip of the tongue irritated Julie, maybe more than it should. But then she'd pulled an overnight shift at the casino. Her eyes burned, and her head was starting to throb. For eight hours, she'd stared at a video monitor—not to catch gamblers cheating but employees thieving—kitchen help and servers, mainly women, wrapping muffalettas or calzones in napkins and stuffing them in their bags for hungry kids at home, a violation of policy she could never bring herself to report. She was hungry herself, and the background music was a little too loud, a melody she recognized from a cheesy eighties song her Aunt Becky used to like, "The Wind Beneath My Wings." Suddenly, fiercely, she wanted to get it over with and leave.

They took a step down to the smaller space, one with a lower ceiling and tan carpet. On a platform in the center of the room sat one casket, two others racked against the wall.

"Now, The Huntley," said the man, running his hand along the beige quilted lining, "is our most popular model in this price range. Real strong, real sturdy." But after the word sturdy, he appeared to run out of things to say and stepped back, waiting, his palms together in a gesture that seemed vaguely spiritual.

Randomly, Julie wondered if anybody ever asked to lie down in them, try them out. Not that she planned to be the first. She walked all around the platformed box, if only to pretend price was not her only consideration. The dark wood veneer, lifting at one corner, reminded her of a folding card table she'd bought years ago at Dollar General. The thing wobbled like it was knee-walking drunk if you so much as rested an elbow on it. And the Huntley emitted a faint odor, a gluey, chemical, headachy smell like the FEMA trailer the two of them had lived in for months after the hurricane. No matter how they aired the place out, they never did get rid of that smell. The handles, three on each side, were shiny and gold-colored, like a cheap bathroom faucet.

Still, it was the obvious choice. The small life insurance policy would only cover about half the expenses. Cremation would have been the cheapest option, but her daddy was old school Catholic and believed in the bodily resurrection, unswayed by arguments about early saints drawn and quartered, boiled in oil, devoured by lions, baptized believers pulverized on fields of battle.

She scanned the price list sheet, which listed The Huntley at $650. "So six-fifty's the total cost for this one?"

"Yes ma'am, that's the total, tax included. But without the commemorative head panel."

Julie assumed he must mean the praying hands and *In God's Care* inscription on the inside of the lid.

"And with a polyester overlay, not satin, like the display model. And no memory drawer, but of course you can put whatever you want in the bed with your dad. Pictures, letters, fishing rods, pool cues. Just yesterday we buried a lady with a po boy and a Bud Lite."

She walked all around the thing once more. She opened her mouth to say she would take it, that it would work just fine, because of course it would. But in the same instant, she pictured her daddy lying right there in the casket, dressed in one of his prized black or navy tailored suits, the only luxuries the man had ever allowed himself. She saw the beaklike nose and age-cratered face, the hands stiffly folded. The worn brown rosary beads draped over those permanently gnarled fingers from all the years of shrimping and trawl repair and odd jobs in the off-season. She saw the smile-shaped scar on his right jaw, a souvenir from the time he'd had one too many and hurled a flowerpot through the living room window in a fit of rage at Julie's stepmom.

And the leg, of course. She saw that, too, amputated above the right knee because nobody at the nursing home cared enough, or had time enough, to keep up with the blood sugar checks. They were easy to do and required no medical training. You could buy a kit over the counter at Walgreens, prick the index finger with a pen-shaped reader that displayed a number on a small digital screen in seconds. She could have helped with that, could have bugged the nurses about it or gone there and checked it herself.

But not from the TV room of the South Mississippi Correctional Institution, twelve months of her life wasted on a charge of simple possession. The day they released her, she'd had her cousin drive her straight down to the nursing home. Stopping at the front desk for her visitor's badge, taking the elevator to the third floor, pausing outside the door to his room, she'd tried to steel herself. But it was all she could do not to weep when she saw the stump outlined under the sheet.

I'll take this one. The words were on her lips. But there was a place inside her, one she had no name for, somewhere between her heart and stomach. And in this place with no name, she felt a twisting, an actual physical sensation like hands wringing out a dishrag, and goddammit.

She raised her arm and pointed. She heard herself say, "I'll take that one," meaning the most beautiful box she'd ever seen, a gleaming, sky blue, limo of a box. A stainless steel casket with brushed nickel hardware, a plush velvet lining so white it hurt her eyes, and a lock and seal—The Oxford.

The man raised his eyebrows in surprise but quickly complimented Julie's taste. The Oxford was his personal favorite, he said, and what a wonderful tribute to her dad. Now, if Julie would just follow him to the office, they'd enter the order so warehouse could get the ball rolling.

In the office, she sank into a soft wing chair and sipped complimentary coffee while the man sat behind a massive desk, tapping a laptop keyboard and peering through his bifocals at the screen. When he was done, Julie pulled out her wallet and credit card, only hesitating a moment, running the pad of her thumb back and forth over the raised numbers. Then she handed it to him.

Walking out into the parking lot, she smelled the rain

that was forecast, blowing in from the Gulf. The wind was starting to pick up, and she knew there'd be whitecaps dotting the Sound. She slid into the Cavalier, turned the key in the ignition, and the engine caught on the second try.

Bzzzzz. Bzzzzz. Her phone vibrated in her purse, and she silenced it, knowing it was Heather calling on her break to check in. She'd wanted to come but hadn't been able to take off work. It would be a problem for Heather, spending money they didn't have on a fancy casket they didn't need. Already Julie could feel her disapproval, hear her voice saying they'd never get out of debt at this rate, and they might as well forget either of them going back to school anytime soon. And she was right. There was no way to justify the foolish purchase. What could she possibly say? She didn't know. But maybe the simplest explanation was the best. A Dollar General casket wouldn't go with the suit. In death, as in life, her daddy was a sharp dressed man.

Tchoutacabouffa (Life on a River)

Ashley gazed through the sliding glass doors, over the deck and back yard sloping down to the river. The Tchoutacabouffa was flooding from all the rain. Soon, it would lap at the cedar fence pickets, creep up the walls of the Little Tykes playhouse, with its bright blue roof and shutters. Until she heard him leave for work and the deadbolt lock behind him, she didn't move. She waited five minutes longer, in case he'd forgotten anything and came back. And then it was go time.

For herself, she took almost nothing: purse, keys, jewelry, two changes of clothes, toothbrush and toothpaste. Into three kitchen garbage bags, she crammed a few outfits for each girl, along with two stuffies each. Shot records, school records, birth certificates, and photos, she slipped in her shoulder bag. The front door cam could have been a problem, since video went straight to his phone, but she'd told him she was dropping off a few bags of clothes at the nearest donation bin.

Her phone, which he tracked, she smashed with a hammer and tossed in the garbage. She'd buy a prepaid at Walmart, once they got there. She'd already closed her Facebook and Insta. She carried the three bags out, one at a time, with her left hand because her right wrist still hurt. She tossed them into the back of the minivan, then stopped. Something caught in her throat at the sight of it—how very little space all their belongings took up in the yawning black cargo hold, all the contents of their life. She swallowed hard and closed the hatch. They needed to get on the road.

She went back in for one last look, in case she'd left anything they couldn't do without. From long habit, she tiptoed around the house, through the family room and living room, through the bathrooms and kitchen. And finally, she walked into the master bedroom, opened the nightstand drawer, and took out his pistol. She could see the safety was on. She knew that much about guns. She held the thing a long moment, considering, before she returned it to the drawer. But at the front door, she stopped, hand on doorknob. She went back to the bedroom, and this time slipped the gun into her shoulder bag. Inside the van, she slid it under her seat.

She reversed out of the drive. As she passed the big magnolia, the empty rope swing moved in the wind, an unnerving image on an unnerving morning. In the cul-de-sac, she accelerated and did not look again at the house on stilts backing up to the Tchoutacabouffa, a word from the Biloxi tribe meaning "broken pot." *Give me strength, Lord,* she prayed. *I can't do this on my own.* She turned on the wipers and headed for the elementary school. They made a *squeak squeak* against the windshield, like the cries of a small, wounded animal.

***

SHE STOPPED AT EXXON to fill up the tank, which should get them as far as Atlanta. Squeezing the nozzle and watching the numbers tick up, she tried not to wonder how long the money would last, which she'd squirreled away ten and twenty bucks at a time. Or what she might get for her jewelry through Craigslist or, as a last resort, from a pawn shop. Her plan had been to save more and wait for final confirmation on the rental property in Myrtle Beach, South Carolina, where Sara, an old friend, had tentatively agreed to let them stay rent-free for a couple of months. In the meantime, she'd cook his favorite foods, keep the house extra nice, keep the kids quiet. Make her interactions with him smooth and frictionless, nothing for him to snag on. Float away somewhere in her head when he climbed on top of her, the way she'd done during both c-sections.

But that was all before he accused her of flirting with Abby's soccer coach, backed her up to the wall, and wrapped his long fingers with the white gold wedding band around her windpipe. Split lips, bruised cheekbone, bruised ribs, two broken fingers, he'd done all that. He'd dragged her down the hall by her hair, locked her in the closet, but the choking was new. His lips were pressed together, nose wrinkled in disgust. That was the moment she knew, for sure, he would kill her if she stayed. That she, Ashley Rose Jackson, would lie on that very bedroom floor, truly and actually dead. Lips blue, feet splayed, stiff as roadkill, and her girls would see her like that. What good was money or an apartment, then?

The road to the school wound along, sometimes nestling right up to the river, now just a few feet down on both sides from the shoulder. The water was the color of coffee with cream, rushing impatiently by. A long, dark branch bobbed along, then a child-sized, red plastic deck chair. It dipped and rocked and swirled, then continued its journey. Just a few miles south, the Tchoutacabouffa would join the Biloxi, then spill into the bay. Then the Mississippi Sound—Deer Island, Horn Island, Ship Island, the Gulf of Mexico. She had lived on the coast all her life, never been farther north than Gatlinburg or farther east than Destin. She'd never been anywhere, really, just here. Just home.

Her mama, Regina, was buried in the cemetery on 90 in Ocean Springs. She wondered if the flowers she'd left three days earlier were still on the grave or if the cemetery people had already taken them away. Yellow roses because her mama was from Texas. Because she had a yellow rose tattooed on her right shoulder. Because her middle name, like Ashley's, was Rose.

Even now, four years after ovarian cancer had taken her, Ashley still had that lopped-off feeling, like yearning for a lost limb. She knew florists delivered to cemeteries and lots of people weren't able to visit their mothers' graves. And of all the things she knew she would miss, why a grave? What was a grave? Just a slab of rock, just earth, just a body. She was raised Baptist and taught the body was nothing, only a shell. But then again, it was everything.

Through the misting rain, she saw brake lights ahead and stopped. It was the drawbridge, raising to let a boat pass, and there was nothing to do but wait for it to lower. On the opposite bank of the river, she spotted a motionless gator on a log. He was ten or twelve feet, easy. That was the reason she'd never let the girls have a dog. It would hurt too much to lose it, and in such a horrible way.

***

IN THE SCHOOL PARKING lot, she scanned the vehicles, almost convinced she'd see his boulder gray Nissan Rogue, that he'd somehow read her thoughts. But that was crazy, and she knew it. She parked, took the keys from the ignition, and breathed. The thing now was just to stay calm, act super casual. She'd picked her kids up many times, and this would be no different. Still, she reached into her jacket pocket, where she carried a small, olive wood pocket cross from the Holy Land. She squeezed it tightly as she stepped out of the car.

Near the school's entrance stood the flagpole, surrounded by recently mown grass. The flag was at half-mast today, popping and snapping in the wind under the low, heavy sky. Her girls had taken part in ceremonies with the flag each year, raising and lowering it with their girl scout troops. First in daisy vests, then brownie vests, and now Abby in her green junior vest, all covered in achievement patches she'd sewn on carefully, knowing each was proof of some small ability or accomplishment that, over time, she prayed would give them the self-confidence she'd always lacked. So much of life depended on confidence.

She rushed to catch the door that was closing behind a man who'd just entered, but she wasn't quick enough. She pressed the buzzer and waited, then pressed it again.

"May I help you?"

"I'm picking up my daughters for a dentist appointment. Abby and Emma Jackson."

After nearly a full minute, the doors clicked, and she walked across the lobby to the front office. The two women behind desks facing each other, she recognized. One was older and short-haired, one younger and longer-haired. The young one always reminded her of the pastor's wife at the church they'd attended for a while. Once, that pastor had preached on marriage, quoting a verse from First Corinthians about husbands' and wives' bodies belonging to each other. He told the congregation not to take what he was about to say the wrong way, not to twist his words, but scripture was clear. And scripture never said anything about husband, or wife, having to be "in the mood." His fingers made air quotes around the phrase. The place went completely silent until one elderly lady in the next row of folding chairs up made a small, strangled sound in her throat. She shook her head, no, no, then stood and walked out with her purse and Bible. The pastor had asked the congregation if he could get an amen, and he did. One male voice said amen, then another, and another.

At the memory, Ashley's wrist throbbed. She took out her license with the photo she'd always thought looked like a mug shot and laid it on the counter to be scanned. In the green early dismissal notebook, she scrawled their names illegibly with her left hand, leaving the return times blank.

"Abby's in Mrs. Dedeaux's class, and Emma's in Mr. Nguyen's," she told the younger woman.

"Did you send in notes this morning?"

"No, sorry, I forgot."

"Always send in a note. That way, we don't have to call the teacher and interrupt class. They'd already be here waiting for you."

"Sorry," she repeated.

"It's okay, just remember for next time."

"I will."

There wouldn't be any next time, of course. They'd never walk these halls again, never see their teachers or classmates again. She'd wanted to Google the new school they'd attend in Myrtle Beach, but she'd once seen him checking her browser history on the laptop, and she suspected he could do the same thing on her phone. So she used a computer at the public library. The school described itself as highly rated and "devoted to nurturing the whole child." From their home page, she clicked on the Facebook icon and scrolled through images of happy-seeming kids, including a brownie troop bagging canned goods for a food pantry. They buoyed her, these images. She could picture Emma fitting in with this troop. She imagined driving them and their new friends to the beach, one with clean water you could swim in without worrying about bacteria counts and skin infections. All that afternoon, it had scrolled through her mind, the bright highlight reel of their possible future lives. One where Emma didn't cry about things she heard at night through her bedroom wall, one where Abby didn't watch lock picking videos on YouTube to get her mama out of the closet.

The woman was just about to call the teachers when a little curly-haired boy, who appeared to be developmentally delayed, entered the office with an aide holding his hand.

"Ian's all ready for the Pledge of Allegiance!" the smiling aide announced.

"Well, come on over, Ian!" the older woman said, and waved the boy to her desk, where she passed the aide a microphone. And then the boy recited the pledge in a soft, lisping voice as the aide prompted him, phrase by phrase.

"*I pledge allegiance.*" Pause. "*To the flag.*" Long pause. "*Of the United States of America.*" Very long pause. "*And to the republic for which it stands.*" Ashley sighed impatiently and bit her lip. As soon as he'd said "with liberty and justice for all," she blurted out, "Can you call now, please?"

Both women looked over at her, eyebrows raised.

"Sorry, I just don't want to be late. If we're late, we'll have to reschedule. So can you just call now, please?"

Did she only imagine it? That the older woman looked suspicious, as if she sensed something was off? Ashley pictured her reaching under her desk to press a secret button, the kind she'd seen in movies about bank robberies. She saw a pack of police rushing in to arrest her for attempted kidnapping, led by his buddy on the force, the one he sometimes shot AKs with on the weekends, just for fun. But the woman only nodded and picked up her phone, called each teacher, and asked for the girls to be released for dentist appointments.

"I signed them out already. I'll just wait outside," Ashley said.

"That's fine."

She stepped out and paced the lobby, then stood next to the large glass display case mounted to the wall. There were trophies, certificates, and photos, all mementos of the school's history going back many years. In one corner hung a newspaper clipping of a young, still pimply-faced Marine, in a big white hat that seemed to balance on top of his bald head, under a caption that read *Freedom Isn't Free*.

***

IT WASN'T LONG BEFORE they came walking down the long, dim, central corridor of painted cinder block, lined with small gray lockers on each side. Abby was the first to appear, exiting from a door that opened onto the hallway. Then Emma entered from the adjoining wing and came along, knock-kneed in leggings and a backpack that seemed too large for her small body. The hall was lit only by two hanging fluorescent fixtures, so from a distance, the girls at first appeared colorless and featureless, only moving shapes. She noticed, for the first time she could remember, the way they walked, the way they held their bodies so tense and tight, shoulders pulled up towards their ears. Whenever they passed a classroom door, they glanced over, as if expecting something to rush out and grab them, sink its teeth into an arm or leg. How had she never noticed the way they walked? She thought of rabbits, squirrels, and chipmunks, and how these animals had an eye on each side of their heads for this very reason. And this image of her beauties as small, furry animals of prey turned her stomach. Dear Lord, she prayed. I have fucked these children up so bad. Only for a moment, she had an awful thought: Would it have been better to have driven up to the Pink House in Jackson, back when it was still legal in Mississippi, and taken care of things? And then her beauties, her everythings, would never have to walk through the world this way.

But no, she had to push that thought away, far away. She couldn't let herself open that door. She whispered the world's oldest prayer: Help.

"I didn't know I had a dentist appointment," Abby said when they made it to where she waited.

"Just come on and hurry up. We need to get on the road."

But she froze when the front office door opened and the older woman came out, rushing towards them across the lobby with a look of alarm on her face. Ashley grabbed their hands, despite the pain in her wrist, and pulled them towards the doors.

"Ow! That hurts!" Emma cried.

"Wait!" the woman said. "Stop!"

But she didn't stop.

"You forgot your license!"

She stopped then. She let out the breath she was holding. She released the girls, and the woman hurried over to them. Her brown eyes were warm and kind as she held out the license.

"Thank you."

"No problem." The woman smiled. "Y'all be safe out there driving. This wind's really starting to blow."

She was right. The wind was picking up, and so was the

rain. It blew in sheets now and slammed against the front doors. The pines waved as they raced to the van. When they got in and locked the doors, they were all dripping wet. She wished she'd thought to bring a couple of towels. How could she have forgotten towels? They didn't even have *towels*. Emma glanced into the cargo hold before buckling into her booster seat.

"Why are my clothes in garbage bags? And Abby's, too?"

The question hung in the air. Ashley didn't answer and cranked the van. She'd hoped to put some miles between them and him before she had to explain. She'd hoped to pull off at a rest stop or a McDonald's and tell them the truth, make certain promises she'd have to keep. Instead, it was Abby who spoke up, sounding both older and younger than her nine years.

"Cause we're not going to the dentist." And in a softer voice, "We're running away from Dad. Aren't we?"

"He's gonna be mad," Emma said, and began to cry.

Ashley turned to them, the engine idling as rain pelted the roof and streamed down the windows. "We're gonna be okay. Things will be different from now on." And she added, with all the cheer and faith and confidence she could summon, "We're going to a real ocean. They've got a boardwalk and everything."

The Waterline

Floyd was trying not to stare at the young lady's nose ring. His grandson, Shaun, had just introduced her as Sophie, his girlfriend. She had short, spiky hair like a guy's, and Shaun's was long and loose, tucked behind his ears. Like they'd swapped haircuts, Floyd thought, a guy's on her and a girl's on him. But he knew the styles were different these days, and it sure was good to see Shaun again. Where was it he was living now? Tennessee? Georgia?

Their waitress walked up then, a Vietnamese lady who winked at Margie beside him and asked if they were on a double date. Floyd liked the Vietnamese, always had. They were good people who'd sacrificed for their freedom, and now here they were, American as apple cream. But wait, was that the expression? It didn't sound right, apple cream.

"What can I get you folks today?"

"You know what you want?" Margie asked him.

Well, that was easy. You couldn't go wrong with flounder. Broiled, stuffed, fried, if it was flounder, he wanted it. But no sooner had they ordered their entrees and two sides, than he remembered something: the plate. Where was that plate, the one Ronald Reagan had eaten from all those years ago when he'd come through here? They'd mounted it on a wall of honor, next to a small American flag and a photo of Reagan smiling with the owner. But now that wall was painted dark green. And where the plate had hung, they'd put up a blue marlin, and under the marlin, a scrap of net strung with plastic crabs and starfish.

"What happened to Reagan's plate?" Floyd asked the waitress. "When did they take it down?"

"Plate?" She glanced over to where Floyd pointed and shook her head. "No sir, I don't know anything about any plate. It's always just been the fish on that wall."

He chuckled at first, thinking she must be pulling his leg. But she didn't look like she was pulling his leg. She looked dead serious. "Course it was," he said. "It was there for years and years."

"Um?" She laughed uncertainly, glancing to Shaun and Sophie for help.

Margie laid her hand on his forearm and whispered. "You're thinking of some other place. The barbeque place, maybe, or the Chinese place?"

But he yanked his arm away from Margie. His eyes flashed, and a purple vein throbbed above his left eyebrow. "Goddammit, woman, I am NOT thinking of some other place," he exploded. "It was right THERE!" He jabbed the air with his pointer finger, anger rolling off him in waves.

Shaun's eyes flew open wide. The waitress made a *yikes* face and asked if they needed a minute or two. The couple at the next table over stopped eating their salads and stared. And Margie looked into her lap and seemed to shrink, swallowed up by the red vinyl booth.

Floyd was out of line, and he knew it. Hollering in public, cussing his own wife? But he'd had a belly full of Margie's constant corrections. The other day, she'd had the nerve to *inform* him she'd be managing the bank accounts and bills from now on, accused him of withdrawing money from the ATM and making the checks bounce, when he'd done no such thing. And she was wrong about that plate, her and the waitress, too. He remembered it clearly.

Shaun stood up from the booth. "Let's talk a walk, Pawpaw. Come on, let's go cool off."

Floyd didn't argue. He could feel his blood pressure

shooting up, and he wondered if he ought to take a clonidine. There was that pulsing behind his eyes, that tightening band around his chest, like a bear hug from an actual bear. He needed some air, alright. He got up and followed Shaun out the doors onto the wraparound deck.

Outside, he gripped the railing and leaned on it, the rough wood warm and sturdy under his hand. The breeze off the Sound blew his hair back. He closed his eyes, and then he could just breathe. He could just listen to the water and the gulls.

"What's going on?" Shaun asked. "You okay?"

"You remember that plate, right?"

Shaun gave him a long look. "I didn't grow up here, remember? I've never been to this place in my life."

Floyd gazed out at the shrimp boats and pleasure boats docked in the harbor below, and out past the harbor and channel to the chunks of concrete jetty off Deer Island. "Used to be houses on that island. Gardens and fruit trees and stuff. Boy I went to school with lived out there and rowed over every morning for school." He could see the boy now, forming out of the air, colors and shapes seeping in like a Polaroid picture. Yes, he saw the boy and his brother in cuffed jeans and crew cuts, tying their skiff to the pier and walking up to where Floyd waited for his friend. "But the big one washed all them houses away." For a few seconds, Floyd struggled to recall the name of the big one, before the more recent big one. Then it came to him. "Camille." So much death and destruction, Biloxi just a scrap lumberyard as far as you could see, his mama and daddy's little house on Point Cadet washed away, not even a stick of furniture left behind.

Shaun laid a hand on his shoulder and squeezed. After a minute or two, he spoke again. "You okay to go back in now? You ready to be nice?"

"I'll be nice," Floyd promised.

"And no more talk about that plate."

***

WHEN THEY MADE IT back to the table, Margie was dabbing her eyes with a napkin and talking to the girl, who nodded sympathetically. Shawn bent and kissed his grandma on the cheek before he sat down. Floyd slid in next to Margie and took a pack of club crackers from the red plastic basket. He stared at it as if he might find something helpful in the tiny blue print on the cellophane wrapper.

"I'm sorry, ladies," he said, after a few seconds of silence. "I don't know what got into me, yelling like that."

"Let's just have a nice lunch with Shaun and Sophie," Margie sighed. "Then you can go home and rest."

Just then the waitress appeared, loaded down with a

platter she placed on a stand next to the table. She set his flounder in front of him, still hot from the oven. The fish was swimming in butter and lemon, just the way he liked it, and the mild, white flesh flaked with the slightest touch of his fork. He lifted out the entire spine in one piece. Oh, he loved him some flounder.

He thought it was a delicious meal. The kids said their gumbo was good—thick but not too thick. Margie went to town on her crab legs, and for dessert they had peach cobbler and ice cream, the best cobbler he'd had in quite some time. And when the busboy came to clear their plates, Floyd announced, "My compliments to the chef!"

But to his surprise, the guy hardly even glanced up, just kept right on snatching their plates and forks like he was in a table-clearing race or something. You could at least acknowledge what a person said, Floyd thought. Even if you didn't speak English, you could at least nod and smile. It really was awful, he thought, how rude and unsociable people had gotten these days, like they didn't have a lick of home training.

When their dishes were cleared, Shaun and Margie were arguing over the check, and the girl was on her phone. Floyd got up and slipped away, walked around between the booths and tables. It bothered his legs to sit still too long, all pins and needles in his knees and ankles. The rude busboy rushed past him with his rolling cart and slammed through the swinging steel doors into the kitchen.

Next to the register sat a rotating wire rack of postcards he'd never noticed before, and brightly colored tee shirts stacked neatly in cubbies. He'd never in his life seen shirts folded so precisely and wondered if maybe a machine had done it. He thought he'd just stroll over and take a look. But as he turned the corner, a young family was eating, a man and woman with their little boy and baby girl. And this little tyke, four or five years old, plenty old enough to know better, Floyd thought, was pitching a fit. He shouted *No!* He growled like a jungle animal, and then, unbelievably, dumped his plate of fried shrimp on the floor. Floyd was stunned, speechless. He stopped and gawked at the mess and the shocking waste of seafood, as the mother went over and kneeled in front of the boy.

"Looks like you're having a rough time, Grayson," she said. "I can see you've got some really big feelings. That can be scary."

The father glanced at them, then back at his phone, typing with his thumbs. The mother tried to take the boy's hand, but he growled again and this time hit her, smack across the face. And *still* the idiot was on his phone. What kind of no-count man was this, teaching his boy it was acceptable to hit a woman? Floyd's heart beat faster and faster. It thrummed all the way to his eardrums. His vision went all strange, kind of swimmy around the edges, and inside his head buzzed a swarm of stinging gnats. And before he could stop himself, he'd walked up to the table, snatched the phone, and hurled it like he was still on the pitcher's mound at Biloxi High. It sailed over the bar, barely missing the bartender's head, and shattered a mirror between liquor bottles and a neon Corona sign.

But he lost his balance and tilted forward. His left foot slipped far out in front, and he went down hard, most of his weight landing on his right knee.

For two or three seconds, the whole place went silent, all the diners' talk just dropping off a cliff. Then he heard a child crying and a man's startled voice: *What the hell?* From the floor, all he could see were shoes and pant cuffs rushing over, blurry because his glasses were on the floor. He lay on his side, curled up and holding his knee, gasping from the pain. And seconds later, Shaun was there, holding him.

"I got you, Pawpaw. I'm right here."

He heard Margie wail. "This is all my fault! I should have known something like this would happen."

***

AT THE ER, THEY x-rayed his leg but found no broken bones, only a sprain and severe bruise that would take some time to heal. They gave him Tylenol and oxycodone and an ice pack that strapped around his knee. A nurse who didn't seem old enough to be a nurse was asking him all kinds of questions: *What year is it, Mr. Davis? Who's the president? Who's this lady sitting next to you?*

"I'm not losing my papers!" he cried. "Marbles, whatever, I just—" He broke off, unable to explain why he'd lost his temper so badly back at the restaurant. He didn't even remember it all clearly. It was just bits and flashes now. But he did recall the cracks in the mirror and the man's voice shouting that they'd be buying him a new iPhone. "I haven't been sleeping well," he finally said. "I think I just need a good night's sleep. That's all."

"Oh, okay," the nurse answered in a loud, high-pitched voice, grinning at him like he was feeble-minded. She nodded and scooted closer on her rolling stool. "We're just checking you out, okay? We're just making sure you're good to go." Then she went over to a computer and screen mounted to the wall, and she typed, *clickety-clack* on the keyboard. She left the room and returned a few minutes later, saying he'd be taking a quick trip down the hall for a CAT scan. Somebody named

Ronnie was going to push him in the wheelchair, and it was nothing at all to worry about.

"You'll be okay, Floyd," Margie said. "We're not going anywhere. I'll be here when you get back, and Shaun and Sophie are out in the lobby."

And he believed her because he assumed the scan was for his knee. But when the orderly wheeled him into the large room with the big white machine, he was helped onto a bed with a kind of u-shaped, molded plastic pillow that his head was supposed to rest in to keep it from moving. There was a piece of elastic to strap around his forehead.

"What's this for?" he asked the girl. "I hurt my knee, not my head." She was a Black girl with the longest fingernails he'd ever seen, but he had nothing against Black people. They were some of the finest individuals he knew.

"No sir, it's a brain scan. And if you move your head around, the images'll come out blurry, and they'll have to run it again. So just lie real still for me, okay? Like a statue. Statues don't move."

"You're making a mistake. I want to see somebody in charge. Right now!"

She walked over to a counter, picked up a sheet of paper, and brought it to him. "What does this say? Cranial computed tomography scan. That's a brain scan. And is that your name?

Floyd E. Davis Jr.?"

It was his name, alright.

"And I am somebody in charge."

It was so loud in the awful white tunnel, even with the foam earplugs she'd given him. Like a plane taking off but never making it up to whatever it was called, just taking off and taking off and taking off. He thought he'd go crazy from the noise, but after a while, it didn't seem quite so bad anymore. The light shining down was bright, so he kept his eyes closed, reflecting on the bewildering events of the day. He hadn't prayed for years. At least, he didn't think so. He had when they found the lump in Margie's neck but didn't recall exactly when that was. What he did recall, strangely, was his granny's little shotgun house with the pump in front and outhouse in back, on a red dirt road out from Petal, up in the piney woods. A large picture had hung on her plywood wall, Jesus walking on the water and, behind him, a wooden ship tossed in the dark and crashing waves. And a man was in the sea with Jesus, one of the disciples with his arms reaching up for help and his face all lit up with terror. In church with his granny, she'd raise her arms like that and cry out, speaking in the unknown tongue. Floyd whispered a quick prayer for help, for answers, but he felt no comfort at all. It was like the prayer was trapped in the tunnel right along with him, unable to rise.

But finally, it was over. A switch was flipped, and the noise stopped. The lights went out. And with a soft, motorized hum, the bed slid out from the tunnel. The girl was there looking down at him and smiling. She took off the head strap and helped him sit up.

"You did great, Mr. Davis. I know that was no fun for you."

"Thanks," he said, feeling surprisingly calmed by her words. "But did I yell at you earlier? Did I talk ugly to you, Hon?"

"Oh, no sir," she said. "You were fine. You were a real gentleman."

***

In the curtained-off room, he waited with Margie for the scan results. She kept wanting him to take a nap, but who could sleep at a time like this?

"I wish you'd just try to get a few minutes of sleep."

"I don't feel like it."

But he did, eventually. He closed his eyes in the bed with the shiny chrome guardrails, surrounded by beeping equipment, and when he opened them again, it took a moment to realize where he was. Margie sat in the only chair, leaning forward with her face in her hands. Her hair on top was so white and thin, he could see right through it to her pink scalp. When did her hair get so thin? And when had she decided to act more like his babysitter than his wife? They fought so much these days, and it was the last thing he wanted to do. Sometimes things got nasty. Once, she'd accused him of losing his hearing aids. But he'd always been careful with his things, all his life, even as a boy. He just wasn't the kind of person who lost things, especially expensive things like hearing aids. So if anybody had done it, it had to be her. She was the mother of his children. They had been through so much together. He felt a pang of tenderness, watching her like this. But the truth was, Margie was changing. She couldn't see it in herself, but her personality was changing. What she'd really like, he thought, was to shrink him down and trap him in a box, like a bug in one of those roach motels they kept under the sink.

She dropped her hands and looked up at him. "I thought you were gonna try to sleep. I'll wake you up when the doctor comes in."

His jaw clenched. At that moment, he was so sick of her telling him what to do, he could vomit. And then something ugly reared up inside him and needed to strike out. And though he really couldn't believe he was saying it, he let go of a secret he'd kept hidden many years, one that would shut her bossy mouth.

"Me and Jean," he said. "You remember Jean from church? Well, we had an affair."

But something was wrong. Margie just looked at him. The shock and pain he'd hoped to see in her face wasn't there.

"Oh, Floyd. You told me last week, and last month, and the month before that. If we were both younger, I'd leave you, but what would you do then? Now just shut up and let me think."

Before he knew how to respond, the steel rings on the curtain rod were yanked back, and in stepped the doctor. He was a Middle Eastern guy, and Floyd had a little trouble understanding his accent. But Floyd had nothing against foreigners. Immigrants had built this country. Still, he couldn't help noticing the man's eye teeth, which were unusually long and a little pointy. He didn't like those teeth, not a bit.

"Sounds like you had a rough afternoon, Mr. Davis," the doctor said, then walked over to the computer and began typing, next to a red plastic box on the wall with the words *Hazard* and *Sharps* in big, black letters.

"I haven't been sleeping well lately. Maybe you could prescribe me some sleeping pills."

"The Oxy will help with your sleep for now," he said without turning around.

"I reckon a good night's sleep would fix me up," Floyd

repeated.

"You might be right. Still, I'd like to go over the scan results with you and your wife. Just give me a second to pull them up."

"I'm a veteran of the US Navy, honorably discharged," Floyd said, though he wasn't exactly sure why those words had popped out of his mouth. "I'm a homeowner."

"Thank you for your service," said the doctor, then switched off the lights.

On the computer screen appeared rows of glowing, neon blue images against a black background. It didn't seem right, somehow, looking at your own brain. Some of the shapes were like horrible alien faces, others like slices of strange, unidentifiable meat, and still others like little curled-up babies in their mothers' wombs. No, it didn't seem right at all, and he had to turn his head away.

"The good news is we found no bleeds or tumors."

"Thank you, Lord," Margie said.

"But this does show some thinning of the gray matter. I don't want you to worry about it, but I would like you to schedule an appointment with Neurology before you leave today."

Gray matter? Floyd thought, picturing claylike blobs floating in jars of clear, vinegary liquid in a science classroom, and the pickled pigs' feet sold in a country store he'd sometimes walk to after school as a boy. Beads of sweat popped out above his upper lip. "Is that necessary? You've already got the scans."

"I'll make the appointment," Margie said.

Floyd wanted to argue, but he changed his mind because what was the point? They weren't interested in anything he had to say. But then a thought occurred to him, like a door opening and a crack of light shining through. And the thought was this: Those pictures on the screen could be anybody's brain. There was no way to tell for sure, just by looking at them, that it was actually his gray matter. A second later, the door opened wider. That doctor could be anybody. Anybody can put on a white coat and a badge. You could probably buy it right off the Web. But something told Floyd he should keep these thoughts to himself, at least for now.

***

THERE WAS PAPERWORK TO sign before they'd let him leave. Margie wheeled him out of the little room, past the other curtained-off spaces and out to a checkout window. She maneuvered him sideways, close enough to reach the counter from the chair. It was privacy this and privacy that, permission this and permission that, and he cursed the lawyers and the government under his breath. He didn't think they'd ever be done. Behind a clear plastic barrier sat a heavy-set gal who kept saying *just another couple signatures, and we'll get you out of here, sir.* When he signed the last one, Margie asked how much they'd owe for today's visit.

She typed on the keyboard, then called the insurance company, holding the receiver between her jaw and shoulder while she squinted at the screen. When she was done, she wrote a number on a yellow square of paper and slid it through the opening under the plastic.

He read the number and, for a moment, couldn't speak. How was that even possible? Did she think they were made of money? "This is—" he began to say.

But she interrupted him. "Y'all haven't finished paying y'all's deductible yet. That's what your insurance carrier says. They cover 90 percent of emergency room visits, but not until that deductible's paid." She looked from Floyd to Margie, then back to Floyd. "I'm so sorry. I truly am. I know that's an awful lot of money."

Margie sucked in her breath, quick and sharp, like she'd been poked in the ribs. But she thanked the woman and said she knew it wasn't her fault, that she was just doing her job. She stuck the paper in her purse and began pushing Floyd away from the counter and across the wide lobby. He was so tired, all of a sudden, his eyelids so heavy. He just wanted to get home to his recliner.

As they rolled over the polished tile floor, the checker-board squares of jade green and white began to blur, reminding him of something from long ago. He let his eyes close, and he drifted back, back. He could see it all so clearly. He could feel the hot sun on his small, tanned body and hear the gulls. He was that little boy again, no older than six or seven, and his daddy had anchored the *Miss Marlene,* named for his oldest sister, off Horn Island, nine miles out in the Gulf. They were near the beach, where the waves began to break, and he leaned over the side, staring down into all that shimmering turquoise. This far out, the water was so clear, he could see all the way to the clean, white, rippled sand on the bottom. He was a good swimmer and begged to jump in. At first, his daddy said no, then relented. Floyd stepped up onto the port side, gripped with his toes, pushed off, and plunged. But down there, eye level with the waterline and the rolling swells, he felt the Gulf for a moment. *Felt* it, felt his true size in it, and a moment was long enough. He panicked, gasping and coughing, saltwater stinging his nose and two strong hands lifting him under his arms, into the safety of the boat.

The scene began to fade, and Floyd opened his eyes. On the other side of the room, a darkly silhouetted man stood in front of the large windows, then started walking towards him.

Floyd's heart leaped because, for one instant, he knew those wide shoulders and long legs, almost believed it was his own dear daddy returned, and he wondered what he had ever done to deserve this moment of grace. But that was only a second because no, of course it wasn't. His daddy was dead many years now, buried in the National Cemetery under a small white marble tombstone among others too numerous to count. This was his grandson, Shaun, who'd always been such a good boy. Shaun was the one he could trust, maybe the only one. Shaun would understand there was nothing wrong with his mind and all he needed was a little rest.

But then Shaun stopped, and a worried look crossed his face. He spoke to the girl beside him. And because Floyd had his new hearing aids in, he could make out Shaun's words. Not all of them, but enough. Oh, yes. He heard plenty.

"Damn . . . take his car keys . . . gonna suck."

That's when Floyd knew he was on his own. Alone and floundering, far out of his depth.

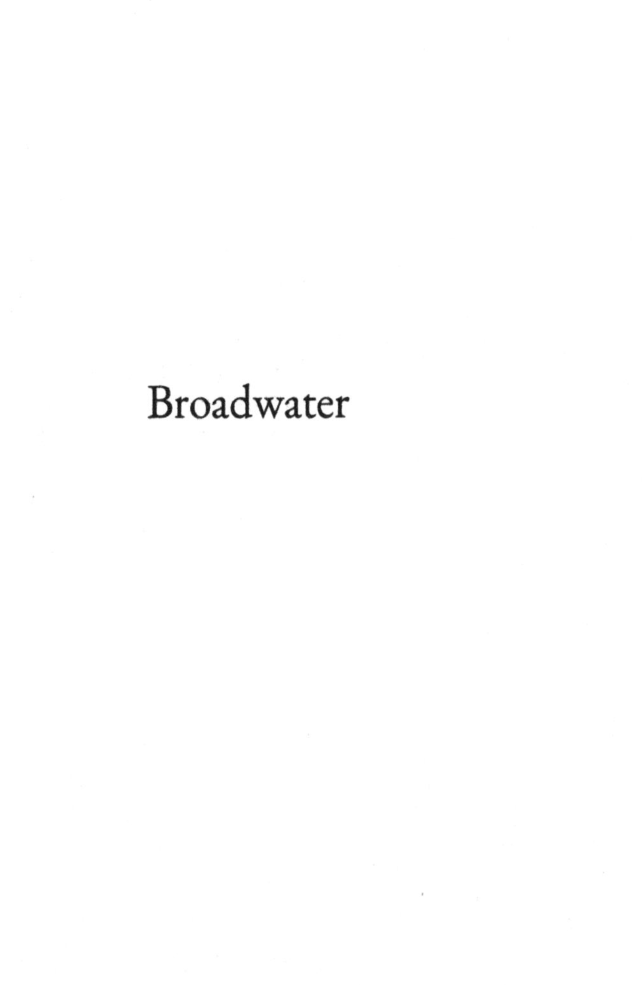

Broadwater

It's June 14th, Tyler's birthday, so I call up the cold case detective. Nothing new to report, he says, but the clock's ticking on that son of a bitch. They'll find my brother's murderer, and did I hear about that CODIS match up in New York State? Girl found dead in an old cider mill, killer identified thirty years later, and all because some second cousin spit in a tube and dropped it in the mail. It's crazy, he says, all the hits they're getting with consumer DNA.

Tyler walked in my bedroom and asked could he borrow a flannel shirt. I was on the phone with Gina, a girl I was seeing at the time. We worked together at Olive Garden. I nodded and pointed to my closet. He took out the shirt, sniffed the armpits, and slipped it on over a black tee. He was in ripped jeans and Birkenstocks. I'd given him shit earlier that day for blowing half his Rouse's paycheck on those hippy-dippy Jesus sandals.

And then it's all how every case matters, every life matters, yadda yadda. But I hear soft crinkling through the phone, like he's digging in a chip bag but trying to keep it quiet. I hear kids in the background, a woman's voice saying *Hush, Daddy's on the phone.* We both pause and wait for the other to speak, but ain't nothing left to say except he'll call with any new developments. I'll be the first to know. I thank him, though I don't really know what for. I hang up, and that's the birthday call, done. Hard to believe my little brother would be thirty years old today.

But those Birkenstocks were part of his new identity. He'd gotten into foreign films and alternative music. He was taking a creative writing class at the community college, carried around a notebook to write down his poems. Sometimes he'd stay up all night working on them. He'd take my uncle's boat and go out on the water to write. Once, he even went camping on Horn Island like Walter Anderson, the famous artist from Ocean Springs. I guess he thought the island might give him some ideas, the way it did for Mr. Anderson. But all he got was bit up from mosquitoes and sand fleas. I read a couple of his poems once and told him they were good. But I don't know anything about poetry, just what we read in high school.

Robert Frost, I think, "The Road Not Taken." One of Tyler's was about an old lady on a city bus watching raindrops slide down the window and thinking back on her life. The other was about shadows, but I got the feeling it was really about our dad.

Couple eyewitnesses remembered the man well enough to help the police draw up a sketch. I thought it resembled Tim on *The Office*, just your basic, ordinary, White guy face. You'd be surprised how many men look like that, once you start noticing. And believe me, you notice. It's like when you buy a new car and suddenly you're seeing that same make and model every time you drive down the road. Only it's your little brother's murderer. You can go crazy. Maybe I did. Followed people, asked questions, took their pictures, took pictures of their license plates. There was that bad scene in Belk's at Edgewater Mall. Another in the Hard Rock parking garage when security escorted me off the premises. One more at a bar in Pascagoula. Now and then, it still happens. I'll be stopped at a red light and look over at the driver in the next lane and do a double take. I'll write down the info, try to get the cops to run the plates. But that doesn't happen too often anymore. I mean, it's been eleven years now. Would I even recognize the guy if I passed him on the street?

He typed up his poems, stapled them together, and made

a little book he gave out for free at poetry readings. He called it The Unblinking Eye, and his friend Zoe illustrated the cover. I went to one of those readings with our mom. It was at a bookstore. She embarrassed him by giving a standing ovation after he was done. In line at the grocery store or at coffee hour after church, people would be bragging about their kids getting band scholarships, academic scholarships, studying computers, whatever. She'd puff up, so proud, and say, My son is a published poet.

I pour a cup of coffee and take it out on the deck. I've got the day off, and I think about taking my Bobcat up to Hurley, over in Jackson County. Buddy of mine bought some land up there and needs all the help he can get clearing brush and pine. That's my yoga, I tell Amber, my girlfriend. That's my meditation, my ayahuasca retreat. Amber's one of these "not all who wander are lost" types, got a Coexist bumper sticker on her car. Lately, she's all about the Buddhists, keeps bugging me to go with her to the Vietnamese temple on Oak Street.

He stood in front of my dresser, checking his look in the mirror. Leaned in close to examine a pimple on his chin. He was growing his hair out, but it wasn't that long yet, just barely touching his collar. Just long enough to tuck behind his ears on both sides like Kurt Cobain. When he was little, it was so blonde, it was white. I got a picture of the two of us climbing on the cannon at Fort Massachusetts on Ship Island. We took the ferry out there with Mom and Marty, this guy she was seeing for a while after our dad left. I don't know why she and Marty broke up. He seemed like a decent man. The cannon's on top of the fort, pointed out to sea. Me and Tyler are way up high, sitting on the barrel. Tyler's in a red tee shirt that reads Popp's Ferry Elementary. His white hair's lifting in the breeze.

But the longer I sit there drinking my coffee, the more I realize I'm not in the brush clearing mood. Not today. Ain't but one place I really want to be.

Gina said she had to go, and I hung up and lay back on the bed. Tyler was still looking in the mirror. So there's this party, he said. This guy from my class. It's gonna be in this cool old barn off 49. But I don't know any of the people except him. It'll be weird going by myself. He turned around and looked at me. You wanna come?

So I go out to the shed, dig around and find the Homer bucket with my granddad's cast net inside. It's one he made himself, taught by his father, who came over here on the boat. You won't find nothing like it at Walmart. Got that chain bottom so it sinks fast, closes like a fist around a school of mullet. He always called them Biloxi bacon. He'd fry them up for breakfast. They're smarter than you think, he'd tell me and

Tyler. You gotta be quick with the throw, or they'll see your shadow through the water and book it outta there.

We didn't really hang out much. I mean, I was three years older. He had his friends, and I had mine. Some kind of awkwardness fell over us. He seemed almost shy about it. I had the thought I should go, that it would be the right thing to do. And not just because he asked. It sounded kind of iffy, driving way up in the country to some party where you didn't even know the people. Anything could happen.

On the way, I stop at the quik shop for ice and a six-pack of Corona. There's one of those bright yellow lucky cats with the waving paw next to the register. Girl rings me up, slips my beer in a paper sack but waits a second before passing it across the counter. Sort of narrows her eyes, tilts her head to the side like she's clocked something in my face, something I can't see. *You okay, sir?* she asks. *Aw yeah, I'm good*, I answer, and smile. She slides the six-pack across and tells me to have a blessed day, and I say for her to do the same. I go out and dump a little of the ice in my Playmate for the beer, pour the rest in my larger Yeti for the fish. Then I leave Ocean Springs and head west on 90 over the bay, across the bridge to the old Broadwater Beach Hotel and Marina.

But me and Gina were both off work that night. She wanted to see some Mel Gibson movie. I wanted to get in her pants. I had the feeling she might finally be ready to give it up.

I cross the bridge and pass St. Michael's, where Granddad was baptized and attended all his life. Church of the Fisherman, they call it. Story goes, two of the priests survived Camille in '69 by climbing the altar and hanging onto statues of the Virgin Mary and St. Joseph. He loved to tell that story. I pass casinos and the schooner pier and the lighthouse. And finally, the little black wrought iron fence and the crypts and mausoleums of the Old Biloxi Cemetery. They got graves going back to French settler times. Our family plot's farther back, in the newer section, where Mom lays next to Tyler. Her one wish was to see his murderer caught before she died. She prayed for it, waited for it, held on longer than the doctors thought was possible. Suffered through six cycles of chemo. It's been three years since I visited their graves. Just can't do it. I keep my foot on the gas until the cemetery's in the rear view.

You don't have to if you don't want to, he said when I hesitated. No biggie.

I turn off 90 and into the empty marina. The Broadwater was a high-end place back in the day, designed by some famous architect. Kind of a modern style, I guess you'd call it. Nothing left now, not after Katrina and the demolition a year later. You'd never dream a place like that even existed. Hotel gone, boat slips gone. Just the plain concrete harbor now and a small lighthouse half-covered in graffiti. They keep talking about building something new here, something just as impressive, but I don't know. I kind of hope they don't, for some reason. I head for my favorite fishing spot at the southeast corner, bump along over dirt and patchy grass. There's a few trash barrels they really ought to come and empty, a few scraggly-ass palm trees. I pull up next to the water and park. I'll have it all to myself today. The place is practically deserted.

Yeah, sorry, I said. I can't. I got a date.

I don't have to wait long for the mullet to show. The water begins to move. It wrinkles and puckers. There's a flash of silver when one leaps up, then another, and another. The weight of Granddad's net feels good in my hands, feels like nothing else in the world. I spin and throw, and it opens like a parachute and slaps the water. I pull, and I know I've got some. I bring it in and dump them in the Yeti. It's eight or so good-sized mullet thumping around in there, couple of smaller ones, too. I'll brine them tonight, put them in the smoker tomorrow with a mix of oak and applewood chips. You can go with hickory or mesquite, but not unless you like your fish with a real strong smoky flavor.

Take it easy, I told him. Be careful. Don't drink and drive. I didn't hear the front door close when he left, just his car cranking. Not like you could miss it. The muffler needed fixing, but he'd spent all his money on the Birkenstocks. I could hear his Fiesta, loud as hell, all the way out to the interstate.

That's when I see them and nearly jump out of my skin. The long, black toes of a great blue heron right behind me. I step away. He's so tall. He's chest high. I reach in the Yeti and grab one of the smaller fish, throw it over to him. In a flash, he spears it, tosses it up, and swallows. I watch the fish slide down that long throat and wait for him to leave. I clap my hands, try to shoo him away, but he won't go. Just stands there completely still. White feathers on his chest lift in the breeze. I've never been up close to one before. It's a whole different thing, let me tell you. It's really something.

A little after three, the knock on the door jolted us awake, me and Mom. I was the first to get there. I opened it to two officers, her standing behind me. She was still tying the belt of her bathrobe.

I start to get the weirdest feeling. It's almost spooky. The hair on my arms prickles up. Watching the heron, I remember how Amber said her mom, Dana, came back as a hummingbird for weeks after she died. Girl wouldn't leave for work until it showed at her kitchen window.

Their faces shone in the porch light. There were two of them, both holding their hats. The older one stared at his shoes. The younger one had big blue eyes. His Adam's apple bobbed once before he spoke. Mrs. Baker, he said, could we please come inside? It's about your son Tyler. My mom cried no no no. My mom made that awful sound.

But I don't believe in reincarnation. Gone is gone. A bird is a bird. And I know my brother has not returned in the form of a great blue heron. Then suddenly he untucks his wings and spreads them wide, spreads them all the way out. Blue-gray feathers tremble at the tips. Air brushes my skin. For a second or two, I don't move. I don't even breathe.

Cannery Girl
(A Retelling of James Joyce's "Eveline")

SHE JUST NEEDED TO think it all through. So Evie walked the shell road along the mucky Mississippi shore, past the wharves and canneries as far down the coast as she could see, past flocks of gulls and heaps of oyster shells higher than the tallest schooner masts. It was Saturday evening and quiet, no hissing steam or clanging metal. She could hear the shells crunch beneath her boots. A big brown pelican glided low over the Gulf. In a flash, it tucked its wings, shot into the water, and popped up seconds later, then sat still and peaceful on the waves, calm as a duck on a pond. But in its sack-like gullet, a good-sized fish thrashed desperately for its life.

As she passed the lighthouse, she saw Kasia Kowalski walking along, too, twelve years old and bouncing one of five baby brothers or sisters on her hip. Evie could remember the night Kasia was born, back in the Baltimore row house their families shared when they all shucked together at Gibb's. Their lives had been hard, surely. Summers, it was bean and berry picking on the Eastern Shore, all day in the hot sun. Winters, south on the train to Biloxi Canning. And then there were her little brothers, making sure they were fed and bathed and nursed when they were ailing. But remembering it all now, with dusk coming on and the palms swaying in the breeze, it seemed to Evie they were happy back then. That's the way she remembered it, anyway, all washed in a pinkish-blue haze, like a picture on a penny postcard.

But her mother had been alive then, and that made all the difference. Her papa didn't drink so much and was kinder when he spoke. Lately, his temper had gotten so bad, she was sometimes afraid he would take his fists to her. But when she was little, he'd set her on his shoulders, and they'd walk around Fells Point, down to the market or to St. Stanislaus Kostka for Saturday mass. She'd feel just like a princess on a pony. He carved the cleverest toy wooden animals to delight her. Her favorite was a bear with a fishing pole. When you pulled a looped string, the pole would jerk up and down, making a tiny wooden fish flop and dance on the line. But that was a long time ago. Everything changes. She was leaving tomorrow with Jacques. They would be married back in Evangeline Parish,

Louisiana, his home. She, Evie, a *wife*. Just like that, he'd asked. And just like that, she'd said yes.

But was she making the right choice, leaving everyone she knew? What would they say about her at the camp, running off with a fella, and not even Polish but a Cajun Frenchie? And what would his people think of her, showing up on his arm? She glanced down at her dress, so old the small white flower pattern had faded into the light blue fabric. The cuffs of her sleeves were beginning to fray. She wished she had a new one to wear when she met them for the first time. She would look like a little beggar coming up the road.

***

SHE HADN'T BEEN TRYING to catch a fella. And what had he seen in her that first day, elbow deep in shrimp shells, flour sack apron buzzing with flies? Magda Pruski had gotten hold of some brown paper and twine, and she'd bundled up her legs that morning for extra warmth. He was dumping his catch from his cousin's schooner in the cart that ran on tracks from wharf to shucking shed. What a sight she must have been. But somehow she'd caught his eye.

Then he came round camp that Saturday night and stood under the big pecan tree between two of the houses, hands jammed in his pockets and shoulders hunched, body so stiff and awkward, you'd think his clothes were made of metal. Eventually, he sidled up next to her on the plank porch, where she sat listening to Feliks Baranek and his son play accordion and fiddle while the children played and a few couples danced.

His English was better than hers, but they managed. He asked about her life and the places she'd seen—the big city of Baltimore and its harbor, her home in the old country. But she barely remembered the village now, after all these years: a smoky room made of logs, the freestanding brick oven they slept on for warmth, the pet name her grandmother called her, *maly ptazek*, little bird. Another memory, she'd tried to forget—her Uncle Josip chased through a wheat field by Russians on horseback and, hours later, the sight of a dog dragging his severed arm.

And there were things she could never make him understand, not in any language: how bone weary she was of tramping all over the country, how nice it would be to set herself down in a decent place, how strange the word "home" sounded to her ears. Where was home?

She wanted to hear about his family's small farm in Louisiana, where he'd return in spring to prepare for the harvest. She asked him what trees grew there. What was the earth like? Was it fine and brown and crumbly, or was it sticky, red-orange clay? He spoke of the wild muscadine grapes that grew in the woods, the sweet muscadine wine, and his family cemetery, three generations of Broussards on the land. They could have talked all night, but her papa came and stood over them, glaring. Jacques got up and extended his right hand, but her papa crossed his arms on his chest and spat, so Jacques nodded to them both and left.

"We were just talking, Papa!"

"Stay away from that Frenchie," he said, his mouth twisting lewdly. "I know what he's after, and once he gets it, he'll be gone, and that's another mouth to feed. I'm warning you, Evalina. Don't let me see you talking to him again."

So after that night she always waited until her papa was pretty far gone on his bootleg whiskey Saturday evenings, too far gone to notice much of anything. And then she slipped away and met Jacques outside the camp, and they'd walk and talk along the shore or the bay.

She liked the way he smiled with his whole face, eyes crinkling at the corners. He had such broad shoulders, and she'd never realized until then that she liked the look of a broad-shouldered man. He kept his hands scrubbed with lye soap, pared his fingernails, even cleaned under them. He made her laugh with his goofy impressions—waddling around, clowning, making faces like an actor named Charlie Chaplin in a moving picture he'd seen, *The Tramp*. She'd never even been to the nickelodeon, but he promised to take her. He said she reminded him of an actress named Lily Halloran, only prettier, and he'd like to have a photograph of her to carry with him. One night, he said he was falling in love with her, and he thought about her all day on the boat. Her mind went blank. She had no idea how to respond, but after a few seconds, she'd said she was falling in love with him, too. And maybe she was. She was awfully fond of him. Was fondness love?

Once, he paid a dime for them to take the electric trolley car down to Presque Isle, where the Biloxi locals picnicked and swam at their leisure. He bought her an iced lemonade, and they sat on a wooden bench under one of the big oaks all draped with scarves of Spanish moss, and when she'd finished her lemonade, he held her hand. A long, white scar ran nearly the length of his tanned forearm, from falling out of a hayloft onto a plow blade when he was seven. She began to trace the scar with her fingertip but felt such a delicious, flooding warmth, it frightened her, and she stopped. But it had happened, that moment between them, like walking through a one-way door together. Riding back on the trolley, they kept grinning at each other. She grinned so much, her cheek muscles ached. He'd say, *What*? And she'd say, *Nothing*. And then she'd say, *What*? And he'd say, *Nothing*.

***

NEAR THE BIG WHITE hotel, she sat on a large stump to rest her legs. A dark green motorcar passed, chugging and sputtering on its spoked wheels, then slowed and turned into the hotel drive. It stopped at the entrance, and she watched a man in a fine black suit step out and open the passenger door for a woman with dark, upswept hair and a fringed parasol. She took his arm, and together they walked up the brick steps and between the columns, onto the wraparound veranda with rocking chairs. The front doors opened as if by magic, as if they'd been waiting for the couple to arrive. But before stepping inside they paused, something passing between them. He threw back his head and laughed, then kissed her on the neck, in the hollow above her collarbone. A married couple, she thought, going up to take a room.

She and Jacques had kissed three times, nothing more. She wondered if he'd done it with girls back in Louisiana. Pretty, dark-haired, French-speaking girls. Strangely, she didn't find the thought unpleasant. She pictured his hands cupping her bottom on a soft feather mattress in a bedroom all their own, and that was not unpleasant, either. She imagined the house as he'd described it—cedar-shingled with a small porch and an indoor privy, an indoor kitchen. A fluffy eiderdown on the bed to keep them warm all winter. Sheets billowing on the line, gathered warm in her arms and brought in still smelling of the clean, country air and the sunshine, no stench of rotting seafood.

She remembered the year they'd all traveled south for the first time, 400 or so signed up by the padrone who'd come around when oyster season closed in Maryland. How delighted they'd all been at the sight of the train's sleeping berths, made up for them with clean, white sheets. But most hadn't even used the berths. Instead, they'd slept upright in their seats all five nights, little ones over their laps. They woke with sore necks and stiff backs, unwilling to soil the bedding with their dirty clothes, their dirty bodies.

How many chances did a girl get to change her life?

She sat on the stump a while longer, but the wind was picking up, and daylight was fading, the edges of things softening and merging with shadows. Along the hotel veranda and in the curtained rooms, gas lamps were being lit, flickering on with a soft, amber glow. It was time to go back. They would be wondering about her by now.

***

JUST OVER A SLIGHT rise, the eight low clapboard houses and two outhouses came into view. The smell of pine smoke, fish, and cabbage drifted on the breeze. Sagging lines of clothes swayed in the wind, the long sleeves of a man's shirt lifting eerily for a moment then dropping. How she wished she could say goodbye to her papa, a proper goodbye. Jacques had wanted to come and speak with him in an open and honorable way, but she knew it would only mean a quarrel, maybe even a fight. That's not how she wanted things to end. No, she told him. She would slip off and meet him at the depot tomorrow morning. Once they'd arrived, she'd send a telegram to let them know she was safe.

Janek was running around with the other boys, kicking a rag ball on the packed dirt, some of them barefoot even in the chill. He wasn't barefoot but needed new boots badly. The sole of his right one flapped loosely, like a tongue. Maybe she could send a little money back, once they were married, if Jacques would allow it. Piotrek sat on an overturned washtub cleaning a fish, scraping guts on the ground then rinsing the flesh in a bucket of clean water. When she walked over to him, he grinned proudly and held up the fish for her to admire. She tried not to think of their daily lives after she left, without her to step between them and their papa. Just a month or so earlier, Piotrek had run off, declaring he hated the old man. It was her who'd found him a day later in a tin-roofed shed behind a church, down the road in Bay St. Louis. Things'll get better, she'd tried to assure him. They're never as bad as they seem. And he's not such a terrible father, she'd said, half-pretending that was true.

And it was just then, with Piotrek filleting the fish on a stump, that Feliks began to play "Kotki Dwa," a lullaby about two gray kittens and the big, yellow moon. She knew it well. It was one her mama used to sing to them. And she froze, sensing the sad shadow of her mama's life falling over her own. Why, on this night of all nights, had Feliks chosen that old tune, if not to remind her of her promise?

She had lived a few hours after the motorcar struck her down near Patterson Park. Evie insisted on coming to the infirmary with her papa, and the two of them sat on either side of the iron bed in a row of iron beds at St. Agnes, the smell of sweat, blood, and phenol heavy in the air. Light fell through a high, narrow window as the priest gave extreme unction, then left. Her papa wept, but Evie's eyes remained strangely dry. Once, when she was little, a small firecracker had gone off in her hand and rung in her ears, and for a minute or two she'd walked around stunned and completely deaf, an invisible wall between herself and the world. It was like that again, watching her mama fight for breath with broken ribs. One of the sisters had given Evie a blue cotton rag, which she dabbed helplessly at the corner of her mama's lips to wipe the thin trickle of blood.

She only managed a few words, reaching out and squeezing Evie's hand. "See the boys raised up well. Keep the family together." Her eyes flared like just-lit candles.

"Yes, Mama. I promise. I will."

She'd meant those words at the time. Of course she had, but it was too much to ask. Did she not deserve a chance at happiness, maybe even love?

***

THEY STOOD TOGETHER ON the wooden platform, under the depot's wide, overhanging eaves. In her hand she held the pink ticket: *Louisville and Nashville Railroad Company, Non-transferable one-way ticket, Biloxi to New Orleans*. Neat holes were punched to mark the date—February 20, 1911. Near them, a white-haired old man squinted through a monocle at his pocket watch. A young mother warned her two pretty children to stop playing and get up off the filthy floor. If they dirtied their traveling clothes, she'd take a switch to their bottoms. At Evie's feet sat the brown leather trunk holding all her things. It was small, child-sized, scratched and scarred from its travels—Toszek village to Krakow, Krakow to Hamburg, Hamburg across the wide gray Atlantic to Locust Point and the Port of Baltimore.

Even years later, she would remember this morning so

clearly. She would remember it the rest of her life, like a moving picture but with color and sound, even smell. The white-haired old man's face in profile, the mole on the ticket seller's cheek, the smell of creosote and horse shit. She would remember, too, the moment Jacques took her hand, sensing her distress, and kissed the nub of her right pinky. She'd lost that finger above the knuckle years earlier after an infected cut from an oyster knife. She had no feeling in it at all and had to be careful or she'd slice it clean off and not even know until she saw the blood. But the way she would remember it, his lips on the severed nerves were warm and soft.

"Won't be much longer," he said. "Are you alright?"

She nodded and forced herself to smile but couldn't speak.

"If you're worried about my folks, don't be. They know you're coming."

She stared down the long, straight track narrowing into the pines. She would be punished for breaking the promise to her mama. She knew that well enough, but would he be punished, too? Would their marriage be poisoned from the start? If you believed the priests, her mama could be watching right now, looking down at her from heaven. It wasn't too late to change her mind and walk back to camp. They'd all be up by now, realizing she was gone for good. She missed her little brothers already.

And who was Jacques, really? It took a long time to know a person, and how long since they'd met, anyway? Three months?

She hardly ever prayed anymore, had lost that habit after her mama died. But in her mind now and in her heart, she whispered a fierce, silent plea to Our Lady of Czestohowa. *Show me what I should do. Give me a sign.*

Down the track, wisps of gray smoke appeared above the trees. She heard the long, piercing whistle, then silence, then a shorter blast. Next the low, rhythmic chugging, louder and louder and louder. The screeching brakes, metal on metal, sparks from the rails. The whooshing and hissing and shouting, and finally the easing to a stop, the great black mass of the engine and the long line of waiting cars.

Doors opened. Passengers descended the steps with their luggage and children. Porters followed in blue uniforms and caps, carrying suitcases they set on the platform or stacked on wheeled carts. One of them, a young man, smiled at Evie and with a sweeping motion of his arm invited her aboard, up the steps and through the door. Beyond him, she glimpsed the luxurious velvet seats, the polished woodwork, the elegant lamps.

"Evie?" Jacques said, real concern now in his voice and in his face. "Evalina?"

Her stomach rose and fell. She just needed a little more time, but there was no time, and there was no answer from Our Lady. A big brass bell clanged, and the conductor's voice boomed: *Departure in five minutes*! Jacques took her hand and squeezed. A wide, winged shadow passed over the station. She looked up, shading her eyes from the sun.

Along the Wires

ON ONE SIDE OF the register stood miniature bottles of Fireball and Jack Daniels, on the other a stack of fundraising flyers for the family of a man killed out on 182, rear-ended by an overweight cane truck bound for the Raceland mill. Greer refilled the scratch-off dispenser case, then reached below the counter and switched on the radio. It was 2:00, time for *Straight Talk with Dr. Deb.* The bell clattered against the door glass, and he greeted the father and young son on their way back to the drink coolers.

He turned on the radio. The program's first caller was a woman whose boyfriend had left her six months pregnant, with no insurance and a hundred sixty bucks to her name. "How could he do that?" she pleaded. "How could Tim be so heartless?"

"Honey, stop right there," interrupted Dr. Deb. "Stop stop stop stop. You did it to yourself. Even a freakin' squirrel knows to make a nest before it starts popping out little baby squirrels."

The caller sounded quite young, which made it hard for Greer to savor her dilemma, the way he usually did, their life-cratering screwups as soothing as a nice warm epsom salt bath when his arthritis bothered him. And something in this girl's voice reminded him of his daughter, Angie. He switched the radio off.

The boy and his father walked up with their drinks, a Yoo Hoo and a hard lemonade. He rang them up, then paused a moment to marvel at the uncanny resemblance: the same buzz cuts and big ears, the same wide-set green eyes and chin clefts.

"No doubt who that child belongs to," Greer said, winking as he dropped the change into the man's palm.

The boy was nine, maybe ten. He stared over Greer's shoulder at the group of photos on the wall, Angie's school pictures, prom pictures, basketball pictures under a red-and-white banner that read *Biloxi Indians*. Above the photos hung a gold-framed prayer to Our Lady of Prompt Succor, Patroness of Louisiana: *Spare us this hurricane season from all harm.* He was mouthing the words when the gunman entered the store.

Shirtless, shoeless, goggle-eyed, waving a .38 all around.

Greer was sixty-one, and Meaux's Gas and Gro had been robbed many times over the years, with handguns, shotguns, a ceremonial sword, even a hypodermic needle. He feared little for himself, only for the stupefied child, who appeared to be wetting his pale blue nylon shorts.

And then—it could not possibly be—and yet it was. This father froze, then took a small, frightened step back and another to the right, behind his son, who now stood between his father and the snub-nosed revolver.

Greer cleared his throat and raised his hands. "Take it easy now," he said. "I'm just gonna open the register."

He removed the till and set it on the counter, and the gunman clacked through the tray, red-brown hair falling into his eyes. He crammed the wad of bills into his pocket and ran out. It was all over in seconds.

For a long moment, no one spoke. There was only the quiet hum of the Slush Puppie machine. The father opened his mouth, then closed it. He put his arm around the boy.

"You're okay, Kyle. You're just fine."

But the boy twisted free of his father and stared down at the wet spot on his shorts. He pinched the clinging fabric and pulled it from his skin. For a second, Greer had no idea what to do. His mind spun like a radio antenna in the middle of nowhere, scanning for any signal at all. Then he remembered that morning's delivery.

"Hang on a sec, young man."

He stooped and took a folded Saints tee shirt from an open box and shook off the dust. It was black, with *Who Dat?* in gold letters, superimposed on a large white fleur de lis. He carried it around the counter and then, as if this were his own child, dropped to one knee and pulled the shirt over the unresisting boy's head, so it hung low and concealed the dark spot.

"All fixed up," Greer said to the boy but instantly regretted the idiotic phrase and its chirpy, condescending tone, so ill-suited to the moment.

"How much we owe you for the shirt?" the man asked, reaching for his wallet.

"Just take him home," Greer replied darkly.

He'd seen an old black and white movie recently, Yankee mobsters in pinstriped suits shooting Tommy guns from moving cars. They tortured a fellow gang member who'd sold them out, a character named Frankie. How Frankie had thrashed and howled when they strapped him to the chair and went to work on his kneecap. Greer thought of his Sears hammer with the black rubber grip. If any soul on earth deserved such a fate, it was this so-called father, who had not protected his child.

What kind of a man? he thought, still kneeling as they left

the store and walked together towards a dusty brown F-150. What kind of a man?

But he knew what kind, knew it only too well. And as he rose, his own leg buckled.

After locking up at eleven, he lingered a while in the parking lot before driving home, staring across the highway at a field of burned cane. More than the blanket of ash that descended each fall at harvest time, more than the smell and the dirty smoke, he disliked those standing blackened husks.

It was 250 miles to Biloxi, Mississippi. He could fill up his tank and be there by dawn, easy, drive to Angie's last known address: Maison D'Orleans Apartments, 2436 Beach Boulevard. He could never rewrite the past, but he might still change the future. Ryleigh would be happy to come in and open the store tomorrow. She would be glad for the hours. Yes, he could certainly do that.

But instead, he drove west, not east, through the desiccated fields towards Thibodaux. A few hours later, quite drunk, he rolled over in bed, fumbled for the phone, and dialed a very old number. There was no ringing, no click, not even a recording to say the number had been disconnected or was no longer in use. Only silence. He began to speak into the receiver.

A Good Home

THEIR OLD PLAID COUCH was sagging in the middle, which kept them at opposite ends each night while watching TV. But with Emily's COVID layoff and Ryan only five weeks clean, they wouldn't be getting a new one anytime soon. They were renting her Uncle Pete's house that summer, a two-bedroom just off I-10 in an older subdivision called Bayou Park, though there was no bayou and no park, only eighteen-wheelers rumbling up and down the highway all night, honking their horns, screeching their brakes, jolting her awake under the wobbly ceiling fan her uncle kept promising to fix. Some nights Ryan would wake up, too, but they hadn't done anything for a month now, since the methadone often kept him from getting it up, much less keeping it up. She'd lie there trying to get back to sleep, but the news stories she'd clicked on that day were so much scarier at night. She'd read one about the health risks of living near highways, especially for the most vulnerable—the old, the sick, and the very young.

Once, she tried laying a thick cotton comforter on the couch, thinking that would improve the situation. But somehow it made things even worse. It didn't stay put, for one thing. It scrunched up or slid around every time they moved, and then they'd both have to get up and reposition the thing, so she took it off and stuck it back in the closet.

One Saturday morning, she woke to find Ryan flipping and fluffing the cushions. She watched from the bedroom doorway as he karate-chopped them with the edges of his hands, reminding her how they'd first met in high school at the martial arts place on Pass Road. The sensei guy, what was his name? Matt, Mark? He'd stenciled a message in big red letters on the wall above the practice mats: A black belt isn't something you wear. It's someone you become. Eventually he made Ryan a junior instructor, put him in charge of the Little Ninjas after school class, where he'd give out awards based on the monthly character trait: discipline, persistence, honesty, courage. A year ago, broke and dying for a fix, he'd done a smash-and-grab on a car that turned out to belong to one of those kids' dads. The guy had recognized Ryan in court.

He stepped back from the couch to examine his work. "Not a permanent solution," he said, "but maybe it's better for now."

But what was he thinking? There it was, the stubborn dip unchanged or maybe even worse, an ever-deepening sinkhole.

Ryan shrugged and walked away, into the kitchen. She could hear him open the fridge and pour a glass of grapefruit juice because he had a clinic appointment over in Gulfport in a little while. He'd found a Reddit post claiming a grapefruit enzyme boosted the methadone's effect, made it feel more like the thing it was supposed to replace. He came back in, sat on his end of the couch, and drank the juice.

His swallowing was so loud in the otherwise silent house. Like the desperate gulping of a person dying of thirst, and she sat on her end and began to cry because if they couldn't even figure out how to fix a sagging couch, how were they ever going to deal with a pregnancy?

"Pregnancy?"

It wasn't how she'd planned on telling him. It occurred to her this would be a good time to pray, but she didn't even know what to pray for, or if what she thought she wanted was the right thing, the responsible thing. She wished she could stop the clock long enough to get her head together before the next words out of his mouth. She didn't look at him but kept her eyes on her feet—pale pink toenails against the worn brown carpet, the yin-yang tattoo on her ankle. For no reason she could name, words from a poem she'd read junior year in English class popped into her head: *So much depends on a red wheelbarrow.*

Ryan set his empty glass on the coffee table and leaned forward but not to pray. He laced his fingers together and held them over the back of his head, like a school kid in a tornado drill. Then he dropped his hands.

"Listen," he said but didn't finish his sentence. She looked at him. He was getting the sweats, his pupils were huge, and his nose was starting to run. He sniffed and wiped it with his wrist. The clinic was a twenty-minute drive. Some mornings, the dosing line was long, and people always used any excuse to cut ahead of you. He couldn't possibly leave now, not at a time like this. But of course he would.

"I'll come straight back as soon as I finish. We can talk then." He sniffed once more and walked into the bedroom for his keys and wallet. "I'm really sorry," he said, and left.

"Priorities," she shot back to the closed door. Then she was alone, with the house more silent than ever.

She'd have liked to call her sister, Lexi, two years younger but already an RN and a homeowner. Not for advice. She'd had enough advice from Lexi to last two or three lifetimes. She just needed to hear her voice, be anchored by that voice. But no, Lexi was working back-to-back shifts at Singing River Hospital in Pascagoula. Her sister was intubating people, texting last messages to their loved ones, holding their hands while they died, maybe at this very moment. Even if Lexi answered, she had no business wasting a nurse's time in the middle of a pandemic.

There was a bottle of Jägermeister in the freezer. She could almost feel the delicious, frosty tingle on her tongue, then the warmth and the sinking down and the letting go. But she hadn't touched alcohol since those two pink lines, just in case. And she didn't touch it now. She took her phone and walked around the block twice, waved at her neighbor, Shane, who was washing his truck in a tee shirt that read *Vaccinated by the Blood of Jesus.* But her walk only took ten minutes, and then she couldn't sit still, and she got bored scrolling Instagram. In desperation, she re-installed Candy Crush, though she'd sworn she was done with it for real this time. And she played but quickly ran through her five free lives, until the hot pink, crying heart with a face appeared, then the running countdown of minutes and seconds until her next life.

An hour later, Ryan was back, looking calmer if not exactly calm. His nose had stopped running, and his pupils were normal. He set his keys on the coffee table. For a moment, he stood in the middle of the living room with his arms folded. Then by silent, mutual agreement, they both sat on the floor, not the couch, though the carpet and pad were thin and made her tailbone ache. And true to his word, they talked.

They talked about the future, and they talked about their past. They talked about how the right thing can happen at the wrong time.

"So you're saying that makes it the wrong thing?" she asked.

For several seconds, he was silent. "Do you hate me?"

"No," she finally answered. She said she understood. He was being practical, and she wanted to be practical, too. She wanted to be realistic. She was going to try.

"But I wouldn't want you to do anything you're not comfortable with. I mean that, Emily. I couldn't live with myself."

Comfortable, she thought. What a strange word. She couldn't remember the last time she'd felt comfortable.

Later, after dinner, they took the cushions off the couch and sat on them, resting their backs against the couch frame while they watched *Game of Thrones*. For the first time in months, he held her hand.

"I'll get clean this time, or I will die trying," he told her. "I swear to you. I swear."

"Don't talk like that."

***

BY THE NEXT MORNING, the decision was made. He took one end of their old plaid couch, and she took the other, surprised at its lightness. And together they carried it out the storm door, down the three concrete steps, and across the little yard of yellowing grass to the curb. Ryan masking-taped a handwritten sign to one of its arms: *Free to a Good Home.*

Inside again, he tried to hug her, but she pulled away and stood, instead, at the front window. The panes trembled in their white wooden grid from a big rig out on I-10, which she'd heard could take you all the way to the Pacific Ocean. To cold, clean water, a real ocean, a real beach. Then the queasiness in her stomach was back, that sourness in her throat, and she knew she'd need the bathroom soon. But she stayed there as long as she could stand it, waiting to see who would stop and take it away.

Blood in the Sand

THE RED LIGHT CAUGHT her on Highway 90 at the Biloxi Lighthouse Pier. It was a bright Tuesday, the sand so white and the water, from a distance, such a pretty blue. But it was the orange canopy tent Tina noticed, shading rows of people in folding chairs, all listening to a man behind a podium. She recognized him as the mayor. Outside the tent stood news cameras on tripods and a group of Black men in bright yellow shirts with blue lettering she couldn't quite make out, their postures strong, solemn, reverent. Then she remembered. They were dedicating a historical marker in remembrance of the civil rights wade-ins during the sixties, when she was just a baby, back when the beach was brand new and all twenty-six miles of it, on pain of arrest or a bloody beat-down, was Whites only.

She'd seen a news program on the wade-ins. A local Black doctor had led a group of peaceful marchers onto the sand one bright Sunday to picnic, toss footballs, and wade into the Gulf. But a mob of Whites had plans of their own. They came with pipes, bats, chains, brass knuckles, even rocks, while the police just stood by and watched it happen. One older woman, only a teen at the time, had teeth broken on that "Bloody Sunday." Watching her face on the screen, Tina's own gums had tingled uncomfortably. An old photo showed blurry Black bodies chased by blurry White bodies, one of those Black bodies obviously a child. She was on the couch with her feet propped up after her day shift at the nursing home. Her husband, Brian, watched from the recliner with a Dunkin iced coffee before his night shift at the casino.

"My God," Brian said. "That's awful. Lived on the coast all my life and never even heard about this."

"Me neither."

"Not a word," he said.

They watched until the end, unable to look away from the photos and interviews. When it was over, she turned the TV off and went into the kitchen to thaw out red beans and rice for a quick dinner. But the unpleasant, ticklish sensation in her gums was still there. And it had stayed with her off and on throughout the evening, like a bothersome gnat.

Now, idling at the red light, she rolled down the window to hear the mayor but couldn't understand his words. If she stopped, she'd be late for work. All the same, she felt a momentary urge to hit her left blinker, turn into the parking lot, and join the assembled group of both Black and White. Out of respect, out of basic human decency, and maybe something more.

***

She'd had a secret Black boyfriend in the eighties, when they were both only eighteen. They worked together at a building supply store after high school, her as a cashier and him in hardware and plumbing. He'd walk up to her checkout line with a customer, pushing a flat cart loaded with two-by-fours and PVC pipe, and she'd get so flustered with him standing right there, she'd sometimes make stupid errors and have to call a supervisor to void the transaction and start over, apologizing to the customer as her cheeks prickled and flamed. After he helped load the purchases, he'd come back in but linger a while around the registers and service desk, joking with the cashiers, his words saying little but his eyes saying everything. His name was Marcus. But when they were alone together, she called him Lovely.

And she dreamed of unlikely, though not impossible,

scenarios that would end with the two of them together for the foreseeable future, maybe even longer. He wasn't her first boyfriend, but he was her first love, the first guy she'd gone all the way with. She adored his dimples, his hands, his eyes, his mouth, even the shape of his feet. Their song was "Tender Love" by The Force MDs. She still lived at home with her parents, hence the secrecy. She'd tell her mama she was going over to her friend Lisa's or Michelle's after work, but instead, they'd go to his cousin's house in east Biloxi, where he was renting a room, or drive out in the country in his car. She gave him one-half of a medallion on a silver chain, engraved with the words *The Lord keep watch between me and thee while we are absent one from another*. The other half she wore around her neck, close to her heart.

But soon enough, her parents heard a shocking rumor from someone at their church. And for the first time in her life, Tina saw her daddy—a big, quiet man with callused hands and a strong back—break down and cry. Her mama walked very calmly from the living room, where they'd confronted her about what they'd heard, to the adjoining kitchen. She opened the silverware drawer and took out a small knife with a lime green plastic handle, the same knife they used to devein shrimp. She pressed it to her wrist, and then Tina and her daddy and her sister, Tracy, dashed into the kitchen and took it from her.

"Please stop, Mama!" Tina cried. "This is crazy. It's 1985, not 1885."

They fought for hours, Tina arguing that racism was wrong, that God made us all equal, that Marcus was a good person. "He took care of his grandma until she died, showering and feeding and dressing her when the rest of the family wanted to just stick her in a facility. But y'all don't even care about that. All you care about is skin color."

"I'm not no racist," her daddy said. "But if you think you're gonna live under this roof and go around with Black guys—"

"How am I ever gonna walk into church again?" her mama interrupted. "Or even the grocery store? What am I supposed to say to your grandparents?"

"I don't get it," Tracy, a high school junior, added. "With your looks, you could have any White guy you wanted."

The next couple of days are just a blur in her memory and a heaviness in her chest she can feel even now, all these years later. She knew her mama had no intention of actually cutting her wrist. At least, she didn't think so. She was just putting on a show, like always, making everything about herself. But in the end, Tina gave in to the pressure and agreed to give him up.

Still, those were only words, and two nights later she climbed out her bedroom window and down the peach tree, walked to the pay phone at Circle K, and called to tell Marcus her parents knew. But there was no need to worry, she assured him. Nothing would come between them, especially not her parents. She would move out or something. Then she walked the six blocks to his cousin's house.

It was after midnight, and she wished she'd thought to bring a flashlight. She also wished he'd offered to drive to Circle K and pick her up in his car, but he hadn't. He'd been quiet on the phone, absorbing it all. In the darkness between streetlights and porch lights, she couldn't see the ground or her feet and stumbled a few times. The headlights of oncoming cars momentarily blinded her, and big dogs barked, making her jump. It took quite a bit longer than she'd thought to make it there.

***

SHE OPENED THE GATE of the chain link fence, walked up the path, and knocked softly, since his cousin and aunt were probably asleep. But when he let her in, his Aunt Mary was still up, watching TV from the couch, a laugh track playing from some late-night sitcom. Tina had entertained the idea, walking over, that maybe his aunt might let her stay there with Marcus, just temporarily, until she could move out of her parents' house and get an apartment of her own, or maybe their own. That had seemed like a possibility. The only impossible thing was life without Marcus. But now, from his aunt's cool, hard gaze, the air thick with hostility, she understood she wouldn't be welcome in this woman's home, that she wasn't welcome now.

"Hi, Mrs. Mary," she managed, smiling stiffly.

The woman nodded once but didn't reply.

"Come on," Marcus said, guiding her down the hallway to his bedroom. On the door, he'd taped a *Purple Rain* poster, Prince revving his motorcycle while Apollonia stood at a distance, half-lit in a doorway. Inside, they started kissing right away, hands all over each other, but after only a moment, he stopped and stepped back. He sat on the green futon couch, and she sat next to him, repeating what she'd said on the phone—that nothing would come between them, that things would work out, somehow.

But to her complete surprise, Marcus said he would always care about her, but this was way too much, way more than he could handle. First all the sneaking around and the lying. Now her crazy mama with the knife to her wrist. How did she think that made him feel? And he feared for his safety, between her daddy and her uncles. He didn't want to be constantly checking his rear view every time he drove anywhere, or lying awake at night listening for the sound of a pump shotgun.

"But Daddy's not violent. Neither's Uncle John and

Uncle Ray. They wouldn't actually hurt you, Marcus. Come on, they're not *criminals*." A part of her felt offended at the suggestion.

In the quiet that followed the word "criminals," the ceiling fan over their heads seemed very loud, *eek eek eek,* fan blades slicing the air. Marcus stared down at his feet, then looked at her as if from a great distance, or as if she were only a child. He took a deep breath and let it out.

"I've been waiting for the right time to tell you." He made a bitter sound in his throat that was not quite a laugh. "I guess this is it. I've been talking to the Navy recruiter, and I'm planning to join up. Tell you the truth, I wanna get as far away from Mississippi and the South as one of those big ships'll take me."

"As far away from me? That's what you mean?" Her voice cracked on the word "me."

"It ain't you." He closed his eyes and pinched the bridge of his nose between his thumb and pointer finger. "It's everything else. I am so sorry."

Time seemed to speed up but also slow down. She panicked, not caring how she looked or sounded with her big, gulpy sobs, with her desperation. "Then let me go with you. I don't care about my parents, just you. I could live in base housing or port housing or whatever while you're out at sea.

We don't have to—" She stopped, unable to speak the words "break up," still half-believing her childhood fear that saying any awful thing aloud would make it come true.

And then she sat very still, hands between her knees and feet flat on the carpet. She stared at the wall and waited to hear him ask her to marry him, to be his Navy wife. Or his live-in girlfriend, or his girlfriend, or his long-distance girlfriend, or anything at all to him. Above their heads, the ceiling fan spun. A wind-up Mickey Mouse alarm clock on his nightstand ticked loudly. From somewhere in the distance a car backfired.

"I'm sorry," he finally said. "I don't think we should see each other anymore. I'll be leaving for boot camp soon, anyway. I don't feel like there's anything else to say."

Tina had her share of character flaws but none worse than her need to strike back, mean as a water moccasin when she was hurt. She'd been that way all her life. And he was hurting her this very second. He was killing her. That's what it felt like.

She winced now to recall the ugly scene that followed, the shameful things that flew out of her mouth. But maybe she had not really said that particular word. Maybe she was just misremembering that part.

***

THE RED LIGHT CHANGED to green, but she no longer felt any

desire to stop and join the ceremony. The people had begun a hymn or a spiritual, something deep and soulful that would never be hers to sing. She wished them all well, then pressed the accelerator and drove on, west along the beach. She hoped Marcus had found eventual happiness, wherever life had taken him. But nothing good would ever come of dwelling on all that. Everybody's got regrets. Who wouldn't love to travel back in time and make different choices, treat people with more kindness and respect? Anyway, that was so long ago, decades ago. He'd probably gotten over the experience pretty quickly. When you're young, you bounce back, she told herself.

She tried to focus now on the residents waiting for her at the nursing home, pushing their call buttons at this very moment. But as she drove, the wind gusted, blowing sand over the dunes and sea oats they'd planted to protect the beach from storms and erosion. Sand drifted above the highway, swirling in pale, wispy clouds. Before she could get her window up, the grit coated her face and her lips. It was on her tongue and between her teeth. At the Shell station, she stopped, bought a bottle of water, and opened it in the parking lot. She rinsed and spat, and she kept on rinsing and spitting until her mouth felt reasonably clean again.

Aid to Families with
Dependent Children

I'll tell you when the real trouble started. And it wasn't the day my father was laid off but weeks later, when Chuck and Debbie, musicians from that holy roller church my mother had started attending, stopped by the house with a big block of welfare cheese. This was back in the eighties, when the government had tons of the stuff sitting around in warehouses. Maybe Chuck was out of work, too. Or maybe he wasn't, but anyway, he assured Mama they had plenty more cheese at home, more than enough for the two of them. Just a few nights earlier, Mama had stood up during a Sunday evening service and requested prayer from the congregation for our financial situation.

This had not gone over well with Daddy. In fact, he never set foot in that church again. *You had no right, Myra!* he'd yelled on the drive home that night. *Broadcasting our private business to all those people? I can't believe you did that.*

So when he came home from the Harrison County Employment Office and found that brick of government cheese in the fridge? Well, you can just imagine. He shut the fridge door, spun around on the linoleum, and informed her we didn't need any GODDAMN welfare cheese, not in this house. Not today, not ever. I watched from the living room with Carla, my fraternal twin. We were fourteen that year. A knobby little place in Daddy's jaw was working in and out, in and out.

"It's not really welfare, Dennis," Mama said. "It's A.F.D.C., Aid to Families with Dependent Children. Anyway, Chuck and Debbie weren't gonna eat it. It would have gone to waste. It's no big deal, Sweetheart." She waved her hand dismissively.

"No big deal," he said. "Sure."

Carla and I thought the cheese was delicious, a little like Velveeta when melted in the oven on bread or crackers. But Daddy wouldn't touch the stuff. While the rest of us ate cheese sandwiches, cheese toast, cheese on Saltines, he ate butter on his crackers, butter on his toast, butter on everything.

***

So obviously, my dad wasn't someone who'd sit around watching the soaps all day while happily collecting unemployment checks. Due to "unforeseen business circumstances," he'd been laid off after thirteen years at the furniture plant north of Biloxi. He'd gotten his start cleaning bathrooms and sweeping sawdust, then worked his way up to Upholstery Apprentice, then Upholstery Assembler, and finally, Upholstery Production Manager for the entire factory.

After the layoffs, he called every contact he'd ever made, from Mobile to Baton Rouge and farther, all the way to North Carolina and Illinois. He pored over the *Sun Herald* classifieds every morning, kept his hair short, and used Just for Men to keep away the gray. Every night he'd drag the coffee table out of the way, anchor his feet under the couch, and do a hundred sit-ups as fast as he could, red-faced and grunting. *Gotta keep my girlish figure*, he'd say to Carla and me, and wink. But despite all his efforts, he was offered nothing paying anything close to what he'd made at the plant. It wasn't his fault, he was told time after time, and it wasn't personal. All the jobs like his were going overseas. These changes were so much bigger than any one individual, and he shouldn't let it get him down.

While he looked, he worked odd jobs, minimum wage

jobs, determined not to fall behind on the mortgage or car note, not to mention keeping the lights on and food on the table. Once he came home with his hands blistered and peeling from some cleaning solution that ate through the worthless gloves they gave him and the other workers. Mama broke spiky leaves off an aloe vera houseplant because she'd heard it was good for burns. She split the leaves with a paring knife, spread the clear goo on his reddened skin with her fingertip, and blew on it. I thought he was done with that job, but the next morning he got up, poured a thermos of coffee, and headed out again.

In the evenings, he'd come home from working like a mule on some construction site and turn on the news to hear Reagan sneering at "welfare queens." Maybe this was why that block of cheese bothered him so. The ugly image was partly about race, of course. Everybody understood this. And Daddy was a White man in Mississippi, not a Black woman in Chicago, like the president's story, but still. Deep down, I think he was terrified he'd look in the mirror one day and see a welfare queen looking back.

And things got worse, money-wise, before they got better. One Saturday morning, Carla poured the last of the Corn Flakes in a bowl and stood there shaking the empty box. I was stacking alphabet blocks with Emmy, who was a year-and-a-half at the time and the reason Mama wasn't working.

With school starting soon, Carla and I wouldn't be around to babysit, and any money Mama made would just go to daycare.

"I know you don't want to hear this, Dennis," she said to him. Something in her voice made my stomach tense. "But you think maybe we ought to try and get on food stamps, just temporarily, of course?"

At the words "food stamps," I froze. Daddy didn't say a word, just stood up from the table, snatched his keys from the hook, and slammed out the front door so hard a glass wall sconce fell and shattered.

"What are we supposed to live on?" she shouted, running out after him. "Monopoly money?"

I heard the car door slam, and Mama stayed outside a little while. Carla came in and sat cross-legged on the floor with Emmy and me. We passed her back and forth, trying to shush her, trying to get her to take her pacifier, assuring her it was all okay. But it wasn't okay. Daddy didn't come home until after midnight. They woke us up yelling at each other while Emmy screamed her head off.

Mama didn't mention food stamps again. The summer dragged on. August came, and with it the unspoken understanding there'd be no new school clothes this year. Carla and I were starting high school. At least my clothes still fit, though. At fourteen, she was somehow still growing, and growing freakishly fast. Fraternal twins or not, we looked nothing alike. I was short and narrow and doughy, with a pudgy belly that refused to flatten, no matter how many sit-ups or leg lifts I did. But Carla was wide and lanky, with big, dangly hands like a guy's. All her jeans were above her ankles, and I knew she'd get teased for wearing "high waters." My sister always attracted the wrong kind of attention. A month or so earlier, she'd tried dyeing her hair black like her idol, Joan Jett. But we were naturally blonde, and the result was a bizarrely unattractive, old ladyish gray that would just have to grow out. Sometimes I wondered how we could even be related, much less twins. We disagreed on basically everything. But it bothered me, it really did, imagining her big, white, bony ankles and the cruel hallway jeers: *Hey, High Waters! Where's the flood?*

***

MEANWHILE, MAMA HAD BECOME more and more a devout churchgoer, mainly alone or with Emmy, though Carla and I let ourselves be dragged along now and then. She started using strange phrases, like "spiritual warfare." One day she informed the two of us that the radio cassette player in the kitchen, along with the car radio, would no longer play ungodly music. I could not fathom how pop and pop country, the kind of music I liked, was ungodly. What was wrong with Alabama? Lionel

Richie? Kenny Rogers? Air Supply? When she played that gospel station, Carla and I would mimic the singers. *Yee haw!* we'd howl, swinging our elbows hoedown style because the twangy southern gospel sounded "so country."

She'd never been much of a Bible reader, but suddenly she was quoting verses at us all day long, mostly about trusting God to deliver us from our troubles. *All things are possible, if we only believe. We walk by faith, not by sight. He'll supply all our needs, according to His riches in glory.* I'd just roll my eyes. So believe me, nobody was more surprised than me when she actually turned out to be right.

One morning, just a week before school started, Linda Pruitt, a church member, knocked on the door and handed Mama a one-hundred-dollar bill. "The Lord's been dealing with my heart," she told Mama. "Take this money and buy some school clothes for your girls."

"But what about—" Mama tried to say.

"Stevie is provided for," Linda interrupted her. "Don't worry about that. And it's a gift, not a loan. Just let me do this for the girls."

"Well, praise the Lord!" Mama said after Linda left. "Didn't I tell you, Kim and Carla? Our God always provides." She beamed at us, almost gloating. But for once, I didn't mind her churchy talk. She told us to hurry up and get dressed. We were going shopping! Daddy had driven all the way over to Louisiana that day to see a man about a job. She must have known he'd be furious about the gift, which he'd consider a handout. But she also knew how much it would mean to us, starting high school with new clothes. Not that she enjoyed the situation. But for her, accepting help when you needed it wasn't like drinking battery acid.

We each bought jeans and polo shirts from Kmart, along with socks and underwear. At Payless, we picked out tennis shoes for Carla and Topsiders for me. So what if they weren't actual, name-brand Topsiders? They looked so neat and preppy, with their white soles and leather laces. I couldn't stop staring at my feet.

As we pulled out of the Payless parking lot, Mama's face was rosier and happier than I'd seen it for months, and I remembered how pretty she was. The air in the car seemed so light and hopeful, I wasn't even surprised when she let us listen, briefly, to the pop station, 94 QID. But when they played "Little Red Corvette," it was back to gospel.

Carla and I groaned theatrically at her music: *Gag me with a spoon!* She laughed and said we could complain if we wanted, but she thought it was time we all had a little fun. So we headed over to the Biloxi Beach Arcade for snow cones. As we drove along the beach, though, her mood began to shift.

"We're so lucky to live on the coast," she mused reflectively. "Just look at all this natural beauty. They say it's the longest man-made beach in the world. Imagine if we lived somewhere inland. Kansas or Missouri or Iowa or somewhere like that?" She shook her head slowly. "We're just so blessed." She talked about these landlocked midwesterners the way she talked about Jewish people, with great pity. How sad it was, she'd occasionally say, their Messiah had come two thousand years ago, and they were still waiting.

"But if it's man-made, how's that natural?" Carla asked. "That doesn't even make sense."

"Oh," Mama said, "you know what I mean."

But as we parked and I took Emmy out of her car seat, Mama's mood shifted again, and this time, she turned to us with a pained expression.

"Now listen," she said. "I know it's been on hard on you girls, the layoff and the money situation and all. But it's been much harder on your father. Try to be extra nice to him. He's real," and she stopped and swallowed hard, like she was forcing down a pill with no water, "discouraged."

But I didn't want to think about Daddy's discouragement, not now. I wanted his discouragement to take a short commercial break. And it did, for that precious half hour. We all had rainbow snow cones, and Carla and I rode the bumper cars, screaming and laughing like we were both little kids again.

But the drive home was quiet. Even Emmy was quiet. When we pulled into the driveway, his green Ford Fairmont was already there. He was just getting out as we parked behind him, and I could see from the expression on his face, the place in Louisiana hadn't offered him the job.

"Just let me do the talking," Mama said. Carla carried Emmy, and I grabbed the shopping bags, two large white ones with the blue and red Kmart logo and a brown paper one from Payless.

"What's all this?" he asked when he saw me with the bags.

My heart beat faster. I almost felt sick. I was so tired of my parents fighting over money.

And I guess Mama was, too. "Oh," she said in a bright, cheery voice. "It was one of those back-to-school shopping spree things. You know, where they have a drawing." The ridiculous lie hung in the air. Maybe you could win something like that from one store, though I'd never actually heard of it. But not from two. Who would believe such a thing? Certainly not him. She turned and took Emmy from Carla and bounced her on her hip. "We won!"

He didn't say anything at first, just stood there running his tongue back and forth over his bottom lip, considering. It was like watching a basketball circle the hoop. He turned his head and looked away then, towards the deep shade of the pines surrounding the house. In a flash, I saw in his profile my Grandpa Earl—his long, thin nose and weak chin, a man so hard and proud, he wouldn't even take aspirin for a toothache. When he was old and couldn't keep his place up anymore, Daddy had once gone to his house and mowed his knee-high grass. For weeks afterward, Grandpa Earl had refused to speak to him.

"Well," he finally said, his voice flat. "Congratulations, I guess." He turned and walked into the house, and we followed him, and that was the end of the matter. The new clothes were never mentioned again.

That night it was pinto beans and rice again for supper. The beans would have tasted better with welfare cheese melted on top, but that was long gone. We were completely out of any kind of cheese. But I was hungry and didn't complain. Towards the end of the meal, Daddy looked across the table at the two of us, Carla and me. His expression, which had been stiff and a little sullen, softened.

"High school, huh?" He shook his head in amazement, as if noticing us for the first time in months and remembering happier days. "You girls are growing up way too fast."

Late that night, well after midnight, the TV woke me up, the volume much too loud. I knew it was him out there in the living room, watching an old western in his corduroy recliner, a John Wayne or a Clint Eastwood, his favorites. *Pew! Pew! Pew!* The rifles blazed from tough, leathery men on horseback in white hats and black hats, fighting over land or women or revenge, fighting to decide who was manliest of all. Somehow I knew all he wanted was for one of us to get up, go in there, and ask him to turn the volume down. But nobody did. We all stayed in bed, unable to sleep, me in the bottom bunk, Carla in the top, Mama in her bed. In the daytime we'd have marched right out to the living room, but nighttime was different, the house all hushed and still. What would we have seen in his face, lit with the bluish-white glow from the screen?

Subtropical Wonderland

Years from now, you'll forsake Biloxi Beach for the Redneck Riviera: Orange Beach, Destin, Navarre. You'll trade the longest man-made beach in the world for clear water and sugar sand, you and all your friends. After 1992, you'll never set foot there again. *Can y'all believe we used to swim in that water,* you'll all say over margaritas at Shaggy's, and shake your heads, and laugh.

But today, you're eight. And all the way down 49 from north Mississippi, you've counted mile markers and read aloud all road signs. South of Hattiesburg, you crack your window because your cousin back in Clarksdale swears you can smell the ocean fifty miles away. You don't smell anything like an ocean, just pine and blacktop and paper mill, the mustard in your brother's Spam-and-mustard sandwich. But the air itself is different, the farther south you drive. It cradles your cheek like your mama's lotioned palm. It fills your pores.

When you finally reach Biloxi, your parents want to unpack, but you and Mike squeal: *beach! beach! beach!* So they unhitch the U-Haul, get the key from the apartment manager, and head south on Beauvoir. You're the first to spot the Gulf: a gauzy, blue-gray smear of potential that just goes on and on.

There are palm trees! You wonder if coconut picking is legal, if fresh tastes better than store-bought, if you really can drink the milk through a straw, like on TV. You don't know there are many varieties of palm and not all are coconut-bearing. You'll feel dumb later that day when your mama calls your grandma: *And then she said, but Mama! We didn't even bring a bag to hold the coconuts!* That story becomes family lore. Though you beg her not to, she'll tell it the rest of her life. She'll tell your high school boyfriend, who becomes your first husband. But Kevin's a long way off. You don't like boys yet. Your mama doesn't cry in the shower yet. Stepfather is just a word. Mike is still Mike, and he will be for years and years. Nobody's even thinking about a thirty-foot wall of water. You are all still yourselves.

After dark, your daddy drives you all back down to the beach. You park just east of the Broadwater Hotel and Marina. Colored lights in the distance twinkle: *Fiesta at the Fiesta.* It's high tide, the whitecaps luminous on black water. Your parents plant lawn chairs in the sand, and you and Mike rush to the water's edge.

He wonders about Deer Island and buried treasure, says he's pretty sure he could swim there if he tried. You say it's probably farther than it looks. You turn and glance back at your parents, chairs so close their arms are touching. Your mama's hair blows all around. She leans in, rests her head in the hollow of his shoulder. He strokes her cheek. At the gesture, you feel both anchored and free. You'll never feel this anchored again. You'll never feel this free.

You take a step then freeze, astonished by the wet sand flashing neon blue. One day, you'll learn this is science, not magic, but you don't know that yet, not tonight. Not tonight.

Acknowledgments

Thanks to the following literary magazines and journals for publishing earlier versions of the following stories:

"The Gospel Giant on Your AM Dial," *Prime Number Magazine*

"Aid to Families with Dependent Children," *Image Journal*

"Along the Wires," *Reckon Review*

"Sharp Dressed Man," *Roi Faineant*

"Tchoutacabouffa (Life on a River)," *Reckon Review*

Heartfelt thanks also to Chris Kosmides and Watertower Press for everything you've done to get my book into the hands of readers. And to Mark Charney, Carol Cleaveland, Lauren Fitch, Dave Heilker, Kendyl Kearley, Will Madden, Meri Robie, Alex Stathes, Jonathan Tomick, Mary Velasquez, and anyone I might have missed (sorry!) from the wonderful Hampden Writers Group, our evenings at Nepenthe and Blue Pit have encouraged me more than you know. Your thoughtful feedback made these stories so much stronger than they'd have been without it.

In addition, I'm grateful to early readers of this work, especially R. Dean Johnson and my fellow students at the Gotham Writers Workshop, along with everyone else who read my work in progress.

To Jen Michalski, Mary Miller, Melissa Pritchard, and Meri Robie: I so appreciate the tremendously generous gift of your time.

Words can never express my depth of gratitude to my dear husband, Matthew Franz, for all his support and encouragement, not to mention his patience and humor, over the many years it's taken to write and revise these stories.

Finally, I want to acknowledge (in no particular order) a few Mississippi writers, living and dead, whose work has amazed, instructed, and inspired me: Lewis Nordan, Jesmyn Ward, Mary Miller, Kiese Laymon, William Faulkner, Natasha Trethewey, Brad Watson, Eudora Welty, and Larry Brown. Perhaps I have no right to even consider myself also a Mississippi writer after decades away from my native state. Certainly, my name doesn't merit mentioning alongside any of theirs. But what can I say? The words go deeper than words. From the cotton fields of the delta, to my grandmother's little house in Grenada, to the beaches, marshes, and pines of the coast, Mississippi is language, roots, memory. It's the prosody of the King James Bible, whose Psalms I memorized before I could read or write. It's the Bible stories, parables, and hymns I learned at home and in church.

A Few Notes on the Stories

"Along the Wires" was inspired by imagery from Mary Gauthier's beautiful song, "Sugar Cane," from the album *Filth and Fire*.

"Cannery Girl" is a close retelling of "Eveline" from James Joyce's classic short story collection, *Dubliners*. The following resources were helpful in researching the lives of early twentieth-century seafood cannery workers for the story. They migrated to Biloxi from Baltimore each year for seasonal work, back when Biloxi was known as "the seafood capital of the world."

Bellande, Ray L., Biloxi Historical Society. biloxihistorical-society.org

Broom, Brian. "Life on Deer Island: His Family Lived 'Off the Grid' for Decades Until Camille Hit." *Biloxi Sun Herald*, 22 Oct. 2019. https://www.sunherald.com/news/local/counties/

harrison-county/article236516793.html

Cecelski, David. "Shuckers and Peelers." *Facing South*."
https://www.facingsouth.org/1992/03/shuckers-and-peelers

Freedman, Russell. *Kids at Work: Lewis Hine and the Crusade Against Child Labor*. Clarion Books, 1994

Hine, Lewis W. "Child Labor in the Canning Industry of Maryland." National Child Labor Committee Documents, Library of Congress, July 1909. www.loc.gov/static/collections/national-child-labor-committee/documents/canneries3.pdf

Manning, Joseph H. "Marie Kriss, Biloxi, Mississippi." Morningsonmaplestreet.com, 2016. https://morningsonmaplestreet.com/2016/10/18/marie-kriss-biloxi-mississippi-2/

Sheffield, David A., and Nicovich, Darnell L. *When Biloxi Was the Seafood Capital of the World*. United States, Biloxi City Council, 1979. https://archives.ubalt.edu/amp/pdfs/R0004_AMP_S02_B01_F011.pdf?

Stephens, Deanne Love. *The Mississippi Gulf Coast Seafood Industry: A People's History*. Univ. Press of Mississippi, 4 June 2021.

This article was especially helpful in understanding the

historical events surrounding the Biloxi Beach wade-ins during the civil rights movement, which helped me write "Blood in the Sand":

https://www.sunherald.com/news/local/article272585882.html

About the Author

Amelia Franz was born and raised in Mississippi and educated at the University of South Alabama and Texas A&M University. She has worked as a K-12 language arts teacher, online writing instructor for academically talented teens, and freelance web designer and copywriter. She lives in the Baltimore area with her husband, three children, and their mini schnauzer.